PRAISE FOR *LEAVE THE NIGHT*

"Want to immerse yourself in a true to life 'great escape' seen through the eyes of an eleven-year old? Put yourself in the hands of accomplished storyteller, R. L. Peterson, who makes you feel you're in every scene of his fine work, *Leave the Night to God*. You won't regret it."

—Matthew J. Pallamary, author of *Land of No Evil*

"I absolutely loved Frankie. He may be 'tough as hickory and smart as a raven,' but he is still just a kid, innocent and caring, the kind of young boy you want to hug and reassure that everything will be okay, even as he faces situations no child should have to deal with. *Leave the Night to God*, R. L. Peterson's latest take on the American family of the 1950s is a story readers will long remember and really never put down. A great story of one young man's battle to belong that readers will never forget."

—Michelle Ivy Davis, author of *Evangeline Brown and the Cadillac Motel*

"R. L. Peterson's work is mesmerizing. He presents believable characters in easy to visualize situations. His rich plotting and wonderful dialog puts the reader in the middle of the action and keeps him turning pages. Peterson's use of language, his humor, insights, and storytelling make *Leave the Night to God* a courageous work of modern literature."

—Clive Aaron Gill, author of *French Perfume and More, The Best Transport Company*, and *The Great Betrayal*

"R. L. Peterson is a genius story teller. With every word he writes, the reader is convinced what he writes is real. His true-to-life characters, rich with human frailties, and the gut-wrenching circumstances each faces, and the settings, baptized with substantive historical elements, make Peterson's writing a masterpiece of fiction."

—Tanya Ross, author of the *Tranquility Series*

"A veteran, award-winning writer, Peterson spins a great story using vocabulary that creates a tale even those with limited English skills will cherish."

—Shu Bethune Wang, author of *Secrets of Words*

"*Leave the Night to God* is beautifully written, almost poetic at times, while providing authentic period detail, and edge-of-your-seat action. The Ku Klux Klan captures Frankie and plans to give him a Firestone Necklace (a rubber tire around his neck, filled with gasoline and set on fire). Frankie escapes using guile and baseball pitching knowledge learned from Little Linda, the Black female pitcher of the barnstorming Kings. In these tense scenes, for the first time in fiction, that my research show, the reader learns the secret coded language the KKK speaks with and what it means. This alone should gain Peterson great acclaim. His description of Frankie's escape, how Frankie uses his moxie to stave off capture is, pure and simple, fine literature."

—Collen Pallamary, author of *Meet Bridgetown's Sweetheart; The Vampire Preservation Society*

LEAVE THE NIGHT TO GOD

R. L. Peterson

Regal House Publishing

Published by
Regal House Publishing, LLC
Raleigh, NC 27587
All rights reserved

ISBN -13 (paperback): 9781646032624
ISBN -13 (epub): 9781646032631
Library of Congress Control Number: 2021949158

Interior by Lafayette & Greene
Cover images © by C. B. Royal

Regal House Publishing, LLC
https://regalhousepublishing.com

The following is a work of fiction created by the author. All names, individuals, characters, places, items, brands, events, etc. were either the product of the author or were used fictitiously. Any name, place, event, person, brand, or item, current or past, is entirely coincidental.

Printed in the United States of America

To those who love the game

When I was a small boy in Kansas, a friend of mine and I were fishing...we talked about what we wanted to be when we grew up. I told him I wanted to be a real major league ball player, a genuine professional like Honus Wagner. My friend said he wanted to be president of the United States. Neither of us got our wish.

—Dwight David Eisenhower, 34th president of the United States.

My pitching philosophy? Keep the ball off the barrel of the bat.

—Satchel Paige, Hall of Fame Pitcher and Observer of Life

PART I

Someone has to lose. Sometimes that's you.

    —Ralph Branca, Brooklyn Dodgers pitcher who gave up Bobby Thomson's home run, October 3, 1951, "The Shot Heard Around the World" that won the National League Championship for the Giants.

1

BASEBALL

Today I die. Today, Monday, August 21, 1950, Sis keeps her promise to put me in the orphan's home in St. Louis. I've slept on her couch, sucked down Post Toasties and slurped Campbell's soup at the chest of drawers in her two-room apartment since Daddy's stroke last February. Now we're speeding down the highway at seventy miles an hour, headed for a place that makes my teeth hurt and my head throb when I think of it.

Hubby whips his Pontiac into curves, zooms down straightaways like J. C. Agajanian at the Indianapolis 500, trying to make up lost time. Every turn we careen around, every mile down the ribbon of concrete, past fields and woods I've never seen before, takes me farther and farther from Daddy, my ball team, my school, and closer, ever closer, to the hellhole I've been threatened with the last seven months.

We're on the road maybe an hour when Sis turns her baby blues on me. "If our mother in heaven saw how pathetic you are today, she'd be ashamed she gave you life."

I don't answer. All I remember about Momma is one night I was crying and a lady with long black hair stuck something in my mouth. "This chicken bone will make your gums feel better."

When I told Sis this, she said, "That was Momma, silly. Trying to help you. But she wasted her time on a cranky-assed baby like you."

Now Sis dabs at her nose with her pink and white hanky. "This is all your fault, Frankie. You're eleven. I told you to straighten up, but did you? No. I took you in when no one else would buy you a nine-cent pair of socks. I work. Cook. Wash. Iron. All for you. How do you repay me? Play baseball, morning, noon, and night. Your rent's only ten dollars a month. When a businessman with money in his pocket comes looking for workers and you broke flat as a cardboard box, you're off playing baseball. That's all you care about. Baseball. The orphanage won't put up with that nonsense one second."

I've heard this same lecture many times. The red feather on her black hat bobs as she talks. Sis forgets that I forked over sixteen bucks in June, twelve in July, and eleven this month. When I remind her, she says, "It's not just the money. It's you. You're a royal pain in the ass."

She's right about baseball. I play it a lot. When I'm digging grounders out of the dirt or stretching a single into a double, I forget Sis and Hubby arguing about how to pay his Drunk-in-Public-View fine, or the nights he comes home three sheets to the wind, throws Sis against the wall, shakes his fist in her face and says through clenched teeth, "Say one fucking word and I'll knock that supercilious smile off yer face."

Sis whispers, "How can I make you feel better?"

"Shut the fuck up, woman. I'm tired of your sass. Keep it up and it'll take nine doctors to patch you up enough to get you to the emergency room."

While they argue, I slip out the back door, climb the mulberry tree in the backyard, belt myself to a limb, and try to sleep.

2

UMPIRES

Sis is the umpire-in-chief in today's bamboozle, though she does have a point about Ray Simms. When he came to hire me to trim trees and stack brush, I was the starting shortstop at an All-Star game in Jeff City. Ray pays a measly two bucks a day for hot, hard work. Selling subscriptions to the *Daily Sun-Gazette*, Volney's newspaper, is my usual job. In a good week, I hand Sis five, maybe six, smackeroos every Saturday afternoon. And my clothes don't get dirty, which she likes.

My boss is on a two-week vacation, so I've had to make a buck doing chores and odd jobs wherever I can find them. Sis is afraid I won't have money for my rent even though Ol' Eye Shade Garrett, the *Sun-Gazette's* editor, hired me to deliver day-old papers to businesses, spread gravel on the paper's parking lot, throw out old newspapers—he called them "the morgue"—and wash the breakroom windows. On the outside. With a tall ladder. Saturday afternoon I gave her eleven greenback dollars as usual along with a bottle of Walgreens "Rose Ruffle" nail polish. She stuffed my do-re-mi into her little black purse without a word. The truth is, it's easier to make an orphan out of me than to teach Hubby to stop drinking.

A week or so ago, I was folding papers in the newsroom when a guy dropped off some pamphlets and an article reprinted from *The Saturday Evening Post*, hoping the paper would publish his press release. It was about a hush-hush program that helps booze hounds stop drinking. The reporter who took the material said this guy used to be a wino who'd pass out in the alley behind the paper office every day. Today, he's sober and fry-cooks at The Grill on Highway 54. I snuck his information home to Sis. She shoved it in a drawer without a howdy-do.

Now her voice cuts through the whine of the tires. "I've put up with your shiftless ways long enough, mister. The orphanage is my last hope. And yours."

She lights a cigarette. "How much longer?" This is aimed at Hubby. She's afraid the orphanage will close before we get there. Hubby blew chunks all night. When I emptied his slop jar this morning, his green puke smelled worse than dog shit.

When we stopped for gas, he stayed in the men's room at Clark's so long that Sis sent me to see if he'd died or slipped out to a bar. White-faced, his hands shaking, we sat in Kroger's parking lot while he swallowed ice cream and guzzled tomato juice, hoping his hands would stop shaking enough that he'd be able to hold the steering wheel. Finally, with his cheeks sunk in like an old grave, he eased the Pontiac onto 54 and hit the gas pedal.

Now it's the hum of the tires, the sway of the car, the boom of my heart, and everyone quiet as a loaded 12-gauge shotgun.

3

Dead Ball

Just before we start up Mineola Hill, Hubby whips the car off the highway, slams on the brakes, leaps out, and races for a stand of trees. Sis and I wait beside signs reading Steep Hill Ahead and Don't Drink: Radiator Water.

Sis gets out, hoping to catch a breeze. She picks up a brown paper sack some family packed their lunch in, shakes out wax paper and bread crusts, and hands it to me. "For His Shitty Ass." Her eyes twinkle. She'd like to laugh.

I find Hubby, pants around his ankles, his ass over a log, face white as the pages of a church hymnal. He grabs the sack without a word. I saunter off to look for squirrels. After maybe ten minutes, Hubby stumbles to the water barrel, rinses his hands, and dries them on his pants leg.

"Kawliga, don't be blue. The orphans have a ball team, I tell you. You can be their star, that's true." Hubby makes up funny names for most everyone he meets. Mine comes from the wooden Indian in Hank Williams's song.

At the car Sis asks, "Shit yourself?"

"Don't get your hat in a twirl, Minnie Pearl." Her real name is Virginia. "With my charm, no harm." He talks in rhymes a lot when he's sober.

"You'd have put Jesse Owens to shame racing for those trees." Sis puts two Camels in her mouth, lights both off the same match, and hands one to Hubby. He grunts and takes a long drag.

We climb into the Pontiac. Tires spin. Gravel spews. We're off to the orphanage at a fast clip.

If Daddy were here, he'd beat the hound-dog crap out of Hubby. *If ya can't handle drink, don't use it.* Daddy's been known to take a snort or two himself, but hardly ever misses work. He fights when he drinks and sometimes winds up in jail, like right before his stroke when he knocked that guy down in a fight at the Blue Moon in Yellowbird. Deputy Branch locked him up, but the sheriff turned him loose. Daddy usually handles his drink fine.

Hubby answers Sis. "Smile, Pearl, smile. Forty or forty-five more is the count in miles. We'll arrive in style."

"We better," Sis says, "or it's your ass."

4

Force Play

Saturday afternoon I was washing windows at the *Sun-Gazette* when I see Hubby's green Pontiac parked beneath the Second Street Bridge, hidden by horse weeds and buck brush. He'd been on a three day "run," as Sis calls his drunks. I climbed down and telephoned her at the dry cleaners where she's a seamstress and counter girl. Sis doesn't drive, so she paid Red Carrol, her steam-press operator, a buck to drive Hubby home, with him zonked out in the back seat, dead to the world.

Sis won't have to bail Hubby out of jail Monday like usual. He's home, in bed, Sis rubbing his feet, feeding him aspirins, lighting his cigarettes, while the radio plays "Standing on the Promises," or "Just as I Am," and Hubby works hard to regain his strength for a repeat performance in a week or so.

In the Missouri Orphan's School and Residence parking lot, Sis says to Hubby, "Put on your hat. You're coming in." If he stays outside, she's afraid he'll sneak off to a beer joint and strand her in the big city. Inside I sit on the end of a gray sofa, sunlight streaming in through a high window, pulling sweat from my armpits and making me itch something fierce. An hour must pass before a gray-haired woman in brown shoes and blue dress leads us into an office with dusty brass plaques and pictures of gray buildings on the wall. She points at three straight-back chairs in front of a big desk. "Sit."

We do as we're told. A few minutes later a fat guy in a blue shirt unbuttoned at the neck, his black necktie dangling, comes in. His face is red. He needs a shave.

"How you folks this fine day?"

His desk has a Bible, an ink pen in a round black holder, a green ink blotter lined with leather, and a sign that reads IN-TAKE OFFICER. "I'm Brother Tipton. I'm here to help ya, glory be. How can I be of service?"

I feel like I'm in Sunday School at Yellowbird Baptist.

Sis smiles, clears her throat, gives her name, and starts her memorized spiel. "I'm here to enroll my little brother in this fine institution. He's eleven. Our daddy had a stroke, and nobody wants him."

Fatty nods. "Spell his name, please."

"F-R-A-N-K-L-I-N. Last name, Walker. As in goes for a walk."

"Thank you. Tell me about Franklin."

Sis takes a deep breath. In her blue dress with round white collar, white low-heel shoes, and nylons, she's innocent as a lilac bush. "He's a burden on his family. And me. Always needs something. Lazy. He could make good money if he'd work, but he won't. Sleeps in trees. Gets his clothes dirty as soon as I wash 'em. Stubborn as a fence post. Lazy. Plays baseball morning, noon, and night."

I'm ready for the glue factory according to her spiel.

She goes on. "Chews with his mouth open. Goes up steps two at a time. Plays instead of working."

Mr. Intake Officer nods. He has small black eyes. Tobacco juice stains the corners of his mouth. Gray dandruff on his shoulders. White shirt, unbuttoned at the neck. Wide blue suspenders with a yellow stripe, holding up brown trousers with the top button loose. Black leather belt. White socks. Black shoes.

"We get lots like him. How does Franklin do in school?" The way he says my name, it sounds like a bad word.

"Daydreams. Fidgets. Chews on his pencil."

Mr. Intake Officer makes a clicking sound and nods his big head. "I'm quite familiar with his kind."

Sis pours it on. "Eats like a glutton. Ate a whole jar of peanut butter. Said ants got in it and he threw it out. A lie. He ate the whole kit and caboodle. By his lonesome. Have to force him to go to church. Waits to the last minute to read his Sunday School lesson. Drops his clothes where he takes them off. Slams the screen door coming and going."

Another nod from her new best friend, Mr. Tipton. "You're at the right place."

Sis winks at me, happy she's hitting it out of the park. Her hand on Hubby's shoulder, she adds, "He's small for his age, but strong."

Should I show my teeth now?

Mr. Intake Officer clears his throat. "Our residents contribute according to their ability. We emphasize daily prayer, a regular routine, scheduled work periods, and rigorous discipline to ensure that our charges are successful here and in later life as well."

Hubby leans forward and sings, "Frankie, Frankie, he's our man. Won't work even if he can. Frankie, Frankie, needs to mature. A spanked bottom is the cure. Frankie, Frankie, ya need this for sure."

Mr. Intake Officer heehaws, his belly shaking, teeth yellow as a sycamore leaf. "That's a good 'un." He slaps a bell with a freckled hand.

A Black man wearing dark blue trousers, light blue shirt, and black ball cap with Orphan's Home sewed on it, comes up. Mr.Intake Officer slaps my shoulder. "Go with Brother Farrell, boy. He'll get ya settled. Yer sister will be along to say her good-byes in a bit."

5

FOUL BALL

Farrell leads me down a concrete sidewalk lined with bricks, across a swath of grass to a room with tall windows painted gray. Inside, a boy about my age pushes a broom. He gives me the once-over but doesn't speak. There are orphans in the Orphan's School and Residence after all.

Farrell points to a small cot with a thin mattress. "Sit," he barks. I'm his dog. "I'll get yer issue."

He unlatches the door, steps into the hall, relocks the door, and gives it a shake.

The boy sweeps closer, his back to me. "Hey, Jetsie. They'll beat our ass if they catch us fraternizin'. Cough if ya hear me."

Is he talking to me? I snort.

"See this." He drops his pants, bends, and points his bare butt at me.

Air leaves the room. Purple and black bruises, yellow blisters, bloody scabs cover his scarred rear end and lower back.

"Yer ass'll look worse than this in a day or two, boy. Discipline, they call it." He tucks the blue shirt with *Orphan* printed on the back into his pants and picks up his broom. I feel as sick as Hubby must have felt this morning.

What's Sweeper's game?

He whispers. "My advice? Run 'fore they learn yer name."

Did I ask for his opinion?

Sweeper points to my paper sack. He smells of onions and Kool-Aid. "Important stuff? They'll take it." With quick hands he hides socks and ball glove behind the radiator's coils. He holds up Daddy's pipe. "Yers?"

"My old man's."

He nods and slides a window open. "They only go up two inches."

He pushes Daddy's pipe through the slit and shuts the window, whisper quiet. His eyes are pale brown like tears washed the color away. "Me and Claudia are gonna bolt tonight."

He moves his broom. "My name is Fredrick T. Oates. Ya don't know me from a dick on a dog, but me and Claudia been here more'n a year. Know how things work." He steps closer. "Ya able-bodied as ya look?"

A silly question. I nod.

"Good. Claudia's my crippled sister. Polio. I need yer help to get her where we're headed. Lights out at ten. Fifteen, twenty minutes later. Peach orchard. North side."

His face is white except for the freckles across his nose. "Deal?"

For some reason, I nod.

"Till then, do what the asshole says. They'll give ya a monkey suit. Sheets. Lock ya in fer the night." He points to the door. "Has a thumb lock on it. Yank the handle toward ya, hard. Twist the knob left. Then right. Fast. It'll open."

He's in a far corner when Farrell comes in with a shirt, sheets, and a scratchy blanket. Sweeper salutes Farrell like he's a soldier. "Would the attendant be so kind as to open the door so the orphan can leave?" He's out the door without a backward glance.

6

Suspended Game

Can I trust Sweeper? I for certain sure don't want my ass beat like his. I want to foxhunt with Daddy. Play a little ball. I figure Sweeper must have a plan, or he wouldn't bolt with a cripple, even if she is his sister.

Where will I go when I'm out of here? Any place beats this hellhole, I reckon. In June, Sis moved Daddy to Kansas so my oldest sister—who I've seen twice in my life—can care for him.

That's where I'll go. Kansas. When I get there, I'll buy some foxhounds and me and Daddy will take to the woods like old times. I don't know where Kansas is, but I'll find it. As Sis would say, I'm broke flat as a cardboard box. Still, this might be my best chance to bolt and be free. I'll worry about the details after I'm out of here. If I'm caught, so what? They can't eat me, right?

I know I could be a setup for Sweeper. A guard waits to nab me. Sweeper wins ice cream or a Nehi, or some prize. But so far, everything he's said checks out. They do take away my possessions. They do issue me a uniform and lock me in. Best of all, when I twist the doorknob like he said, it opens on my third try.

I lie on the floor and watch the tall windows. Sis won't come say goodbye. I'm on my own, I figure.

I open the door a crack and sit with my back against the cot waiting for the hallway lights to go out. I hear kids' voices but can't make out words. After a while, the windows grow darker. Sundown, I figure. All's quiet. I stretch out on the floor. This feels good. My eyes grow heavy. I'll rest them a minute.

The hall lights flicker off, then on, then go dark. I jerk awake, afraid I've overslept. I sit up, stuff socks and underwear into my Johnny Pesky ball glove, hang it from my belt, slip Daddy's pipe under my shirt, and ease into the hall. Four quick steps take me to the double doors.

A thick chain snakes through the handles; a padlock gleams. I lean against the chain. It clinks and goes slack a few inches. I squeeze through.

The shadows on the porch are dark. Nothing moves. The only sound is the boom of my heart. I drop to my knees and peek around the corner. A wide lawn. Two buildings. Tall fence at the far end. Waning moon. Black trees against a black sky. The peach orchard?

I slip from shadow to shadow for forty, fifty yards. Then like I'm running out a bunt, I dash for a clump of trees and press myself against a trunk. I don't know where Sweeper is or if I'm where I should be.

A lightbulb, dim as a dying firefly, swings in the breeze above a high fence. I worry that Sweeper and his sister took off without me. A chill like spider tracks runs up my back. A breeze teases the trees. Night birds twitter. I'm breathing fast.

A month of Sundays passes. No Sweeper. The night is root-cellar dark. I tell myself that I'll count to 500, and if he doesn't show, I'll sneak back to my room and bolt some other day.

"Three hundred ninety-six. Three hundred ninety-seven. Three hundred ninety-eight." A whip-poor-will calls. An owl hoots. A dove coos. No Sweeper. "Four hundred ninety-eight. Four hundred ninety-nine. Five hundred."

A two-story building looms black against the sky. A dark shadow presses my ear. "This is south, boy, not north." It's Sweeper. He shoves a sack at me. "Sandwiches. Apples. Yer on yer own, Jetsie. Claudia's in the infirmary. We cain't bolt tonight. Ya got mebbe five fuckin' minutes 'fore the night watchman comes by. Foundation rock two over from the second window is loose. Push it aside. Wiggle in. Pull it back so me and Claudia can go out the same way, someday. Crawl to the far side. Oleanders mean yer on the street. Run west to the railroad tracks."

He pushes me into the night.

PART II

If I could throw an invisible ball, a disappearing curve, or a burning hot fast ball, I would, I tell you. Hell, the batter is out to murder everything I throw, so why can't I use a trick or two to get the SOB out?

> —Harvey Haddox, Major League pitcher who threw fourteen innings of no-hit baseball and still lost the game.

7

INFIELD FLY

Railroad ties are easier to walk on than dodging tree limbs in dark woods, I figure, so I follow the track. I don't know where I'm going, how I'll get there, or what I'll eat on the way. I'm flat busted. I reckon the orphanage won't know I'm gone till morning and the room they locked me in is empty. By then I hope to be ten, maybe fifteen miles away. Come morning, I'll find out where Kansas is and go there in a hurry.

A train track crosses a long bridge. A crooked moon floats in black water. Whip-poor-wills and bats swoop. Frogs croak. Dew settling on the ties makes them hard to walk on. The smell of creosote and weeds is strong. It's a long fall to the river, so I don't look down.

I distract myself by thinking of my favorite ball team, the St. Louis Cardinals. I wonder who they played today. I can see it now. The famous Stan Musial's at bat. He wiggles his hips as the pitcher winds, swings his bat in a pretty arc, and sends a curveball deep into the right-field seats. That's what I'll do someday. Play ball for the Cards. Hit left-handed. Bat cleanup. Bust home runs.

I'm up. Bases loaded. Ninth inning. Two outs. Cards down by three to the Boston Braves. Warren Spahn pitching. I rub my hands with dirt, take a practice swing, and watch his fastball come in, low and away. Ball one. He fires again. Curve. Strike one.

Now I can swing. Spahn winds and pitches—fastball, inside, knee high. I barrel up that ball and send it soaring deep into the night, disappearing in the seats. Cardinals win!

The crowd rumbles. A fan waves a bright light in big circles. A train whistle blows. The light grows brighter and brighter, excited fans roar.

The ground shakes. The whistle screams, closer this time. I look over my shoulder.

A train barrels down on me from the darkness. I dive into weeds. Hot air blasts my face. My scalp tingles. Silver wheels flash inches from my eyes. Rocks and sticks pelt my face. The train screeches into the night. My hands shake. I can't swallow. My ball cap floats and twirls against the dark sky, headed for the river below. *You almost bought the farm, Walker. Stay awake, boy.*

8

OBSTRUCTION

Most folks think foxhunting is men in red coats on horseback, leaping fallen trees and jumping fences, just to watch a pack of dogs tear a poor fox to shreds with their fangs. That's not how me and Daddy hunted.

We turned our hounds loose in the woods, usually around sundown, at least twice a week. The dogs ran in big circles, their noses to the ground. When they scented a fox, they barked. We called that *giving mouth*. The closer they got to the fox, the more mouth they gave.

Daddy and me liked to hear our hounds drive a red fox along a ridgeline, giving mouth every time their feet hit the ground, the sound echoing up the hollow and through the trees, mellow and pretty as moonlight.

"Dinah's sweet as a Liberty Bell, ain't she? Like she's roped to Ol' Red," Daddy'd say. He was partial to Walker foxhounds because they're easier to see at night since they're mostly white with lemon and tan markings. Some hunters run Goodman, July, or Twigg hounds. They're more often brown and black, a hand or two smaller than Walkers.

Daddy had only three hounds. He'd hoped to get more come fall. When we hunted, it was with Stub and his coarse bawl, Little Bit with her turkey gobble, and Dinah's ringing-bell chop. They'd run Mr. Fox up the creek bottom and over the hill with Daddy and me busting through buck brush and blackberry vines, chasing after them by the light of the moon. Some nights Red ran in a big circle for maybe four or five hours. Other times, it was a beeline for the next county. Wherever the fox and our hounds went, Daddy and I ran after 'em.

We never killed a fox. "They like to run, so we'll chase it

'nother night," Daddy said. By the time Mr. Fox holed up, the sun was peeking through the trees. Daddy blew his horn. The dogs came in one by one, whining, bellies rubbing the ground, sweaty, muddy, ready to go home.

The old chicken house was our dog kennel. I watered the hounds, broke cornbread into each bowl, added a cup of dry dog food, splashed in Carnation milk, and stirred. While they ate, Daddy ran his hands over each hound, looking for ticks, cockle burrs, and cuts. He'd check their paws for torn nails, blisters, and briars. He'd daub coal oil and sugar on a gash, put rubbing alcohol on ticks, and flick them into a pie pan that he set on fire once each dog was ticked.

The hounds cared for, Daddy and me would peel off our clothes and slosh cold water over each other, drying off with Army surplus towels. Summertime, I'd raise my arms and spread my legs. Daddy'd look me over for ticks and slap rubbing alcohol on chigger and mosquito bites. If school was in, I'd change into overalls, scarf down oatmeal covered with Karo syrup, and trot off to school, hoping to get there in time to read aloud. Some days my breakfast was leftover navy beans and cornbread. Other times it was tomatoes and sauerkraut. If Daddy had sold a load of wood or plowed a garden or cut a field of hay, we'd chow down on Spam with Holsum bread smothered in Karo.

If somehow a hen or two escaped the chicken hawks, foxes, and snakes, we'd have eggs most meals. We didn't own a cow or have indoor plumbing, running water, or electricity, though Daddy said come spring, when the power line was close enough, we'd join the co-op and have electric lights in the house.

Most every Saturday night a gaggle of hunters—Daddy called 'em Cinderellas—turned their hounds loose in the woods along Layer Creek east of our house where I could take you to at least three fox dens. These guys built a fire, talked crops, and gossiped. Every so often they'd walk up on the ridge to hear the hounds run. Long about midnight they'd put out the fire, call in their dogs, and head home.

"That ain't my kinda huntin'," Daddy said. "I like goin' where my hounds go." He was what you call a hard hunter.

If Daddy was asked what crops he grew, he'd answer, "Foxhounds and foxhunters. I may not win a Good Housekeeping Seal of Approval as a parent, but by God, my boy can take care of hisself in the woods." That I could.

Daddy liked living where we did. "We got an honest landlord who don't mind if I sell a cord of firewood now and then to buy groceries or a pint of whiskey. Plus, we got three good year-round springs right close, so we got no worries 'bout water. Yer school's, what, a mile away? We got it good, boy."

While I was in school, Daddy'd harness Jim and Jude, our mules, and drag a log or two to the wood lot and cut it into firewood. Sometimes he'd rick up what he'd already cut so it would dry and bring a good price come fall. Some days he'd ride Jim to town for a beer or two at the Blue Moon and get home after dark, or maybe the next day.

Momma died when I was four. I don't remember much about Momma, except that she slept a lot. I had to tiptoe and whisper when allowed in her room. Once, she stayed in bed when I came in. She asked me to hold her hand while she slept. After maybe two hours she turned over and let go of my fingers. I snuck out before she could grab me again. Not long after that, some men took came and took her away in a long black car. She never came back.

My oldest sister, Carolina, was married and gone before I was born. Virginia, eight years older than me, did our washing and ironing on weekends and went to school weekdays, often leaving before light in the morning and coming home after dark. Two years ago she moved to Volney, leaving Daddy and me to batch alone on forty acres of rented land.

Before his stroke, when the moon hung low and stars were being born and a breeze danced in the trees, me and him would grab our hounds and head for the woods, chasing twelve or fifteen miles through scrub oaks and hickory saplings, the sun a red ball in the east 'fore we called it a night.

Daddy bragged all the time 'bout how good a foxhound Dinah was. *Best I ever seen. If 'n we find the right stud, we'll breed her come fall. She'll whelp some fine pups.* His stroke happened before he found her perfect mate.

9

IN THE HOLE

I read in *The Hunter's Horn,* the foxhunting magazine Daddy read cover to cover every month, that the best way to follow your pack without wearing yourself to a frazzle was to walk a hundred steps, then run a hundred. Walk. Then run. That's what I do now, keeping my eyes four or five railroad ties ahead, my legs pumping, my lungs working, my heart 'bout to come out of my chest.

I can't take a break. If the sheriff grabs me, he'll haul me back to the orphanage and they'll beat my ass raw like they did Sweeper's. I walk, then run, past wheat fields and farmhouses that look like toys in the moonlight, past cornfields and hay fields, cows in pastures and horses under tall trees. My legs ache, my chest burns, but I keep going, the moon at my back, stars cold and lonely looking.

I wonder if Sis got Hubby home sober. If I were at her apartment, I'd climb the mulberry tree next to the driveway, find a safe limb, and sleep. But she doesn't want me.

Passing a big barn, the smell of fresh hay and manure reminds me of when I'd help Daddy feed the steers he raised on shares. We'd spread their hay, then sit in the wagon as the mules rested. Daddy'd take out his pipe, tamp in Golden Grain tobacco, and light up, blue smoke circling his straw hat, mingling with the scent of cows, mule sweat, and fresh spread hay.

I yawn, my eyes sting. I don't know how far I am from the orphanage, but I'm tired. A tall tree in a grassy field calls to me.

I trot across the pasture, dodging cows and cow pies. Fifteen or twenty feet away, I can tell it's an oak. I run, jump high, grab rough bark, shimmy to a low limb, and pull myself into my bedroom.

In the bough, belted to a limb, the breeze cools my sweat, causing me to shiver. Mosquitoes dive-bomb my ears and neck. I swat gnats and gobble the last of the PB & J sandwiches and the tiny apple Sweeper gave me. I worry about hornet's nests, snakes, and black widow spiders. My arm throbs where I scraped it when I fell.

I rub Daddy's pipe on my cheek. The tree sways. An owl hoots. A dove coos. My eyes close. Silent silver stars march in the gray sky.

I sleep.

10

BARNSTORMING

Squabbling crows pull me awake. The sun hurts my eyes. Cows drink at a partly fenced pond below me. Butterflies flit in the weeds. A red squirrel scampers toward a stand of hickory trees. My face stings from mosquito bites; my arms itch. A north-south road runs beneath a water tower toward some buildings huddled under tall maples.

I could eat a mule, but I'm flat broke.

I drop to the ground. My feet and legs hurt. I hope I can find enough empty soda bottles in the grass to pay for breakfast. A glass bottle is worth two cents. Folks often throw out empties at stop signs.

The grass is knee high, wet with dew. There's a Coke bottle! A Nehi! I'm in luck. I stuff eight empties under my belt. A sign reads, BELLVILLE, POPULATION 31,407. I think Bellville is in Illinois.

The road leads to a grocery store, a rooming house, a feed store, and a blacksmith shop. A DRINK COCA COLA sign in the store window gives hours: 7:00 a.m. to 8:00 p.m., Monday thru Saturday.

A yellow handbill on an electric pole catches my eye. *Exciting Baseball! Watch your hometown heroes play the Kansas City River Kings and Mississippi Mud Dog All Stars this Saturday and Sunday afternoon.* In a drawing of a baseball, are the words, *Can Suitcase Paine, America's Number One Pitcher, Larruping Lloyd Gates, World Home Run King, and Sudden Sam Crosby, the Fastest Human on Two Legs, beat your locals? Come root your boys to victory. Admission: 50 cents.*

Under a picture of a pitcher, it reads, *FREE pitching demon-stration Friday afternoon. Get a hit off Little Linda Lou, America's only Professional Female Hurler, and win BIG money. August 14, 15 and 16.*

That was two weeks ago. I wish I could've seen Sudden Sam run the bases. Speed and bunts are my kinda game.

A man in a white shirt, his tie hanging loose, wearing suit pants with no jacket, comes out of the boardinghouse, crosses the street, and climbs the store's steps. He sees me reading the handbill. "Ever watch them coloreds play? Quite a show. Ground ball to shortstop, they're liable to flip it to third, then home, and still throw the runner out. I seen this Gates guy lay his bat across home plate for two strikes. The next pitch on the way, he grabbed his Shelagh and socked that ball five hundred feet. It ain't real baseball but entertainin' if ya like coloreds makin' fools of themselves."

He slides onto the bench along the wall.

"Barnstormin's 'bout dead since that Black college boy, Jack Robinson, hooked on with the Dodgers." He eyes the ball glove at my belt but doesn't ask about it. "The Kings are smart for coloreds. Play local teams. Keep the score low the first game so folks'll buy tickets for the next one, hopin' the home team will win. To cut expenses, the colored team camps out in nearby pastures. That gal pitcher does they's cookin'. Travel from town to town in a big purple car."

This is interesting, but I'm worried about my next meal. I catch a glimpse of myself in the store window. If Sis were here, she'd slap me silly. I'm dirty as a railroad hobo.

Then I remember, I am one.

11

Spectator Interference

A boy, a couple of years older and a lot taller than me, wearing a green bow tie, a long white apron, and shiny brown shoes, steps out on the porch. "We're open." Like he's a radio announcer or somebody important.

Inside, I hand him my bottles. He gives me the stink eye, shakes his head, and disappears through a swinging door. Mr. Black Baseball Expert grabs a roll of Tums, a pack of cigarettes, and a box of cough drops and stands by the cash register.

When Boy Helper comes up, I say to the man in glasses, white shirt, and long blue tie, who I take to be the store owner or boss, "Dime's worth of baloney, please."

Boy Helper says, "He turned in sixteen bottles. One we couldn't take. That's thirty cents." Before I can say he counted wrong, he disappears through the swinging door.

"A nickel more buys a half-pound," the boss says.

Mr. Black Baseball Expert says, "Give him a half pound, Carl. Loaf of bread. Sack of them potato chips. RC Cola. On my tab. He's a ballplayer, can't ya see? Carries his glove with him in case a game breaks out."

They both laugh. Loud.

"Thanks." My face goes hot. My ears ring. I stumble outside.

Mr. Black Baseball Expert comes out a few minutes later. "Ya got tar all over ya. How come?"

I look at my pants. Black goo from waist to legs, shirt creosote streaked. "Helping Daddy put on a new roof."

"That a fact? Finish early?"

"No, sir. Ran out of nails. That's what I'm here for. We'll finish up when Daddy's home from work."

"Where's he work?"

I saw a sign on a fence post advertising Bellville Coal and Fuel last night. "Bellville Coal."

"That a fact? Thought they sold coal but didn't mine it."

"Daddy drives a truck." I'm scrambling. *All Daddy knows how to drive is a team of mules.*

"That a fact? Thought I knew ever driver there." His brown eyes lock on mine. "This roof job. Where's it at?"

He's sure nosy. "The old Smith place." My sandwich goes dry in my mouth. "Daddy bought it last fall."

"That a fact? Don't know the Smith place, an' it's my business to know who farms what from here to Cape Girardeau." He takes off his hat. "What's your name, son?"

"Stan." Mr. Musial won't mind if I borrow his first name, will he?

"Stan, from the smell, that's creosote on ya, not tar. Ya ain't got money to buy breakfast, much less roofin' nails. Ya look like ya been shot at and missed, shit at and hit. What's the deal?"

I watch his face. Sis said I lie when I should tell the truth. I take a deep breath, my throat aching. "Name's Frankie Walker. I'm eleven. Momma died when I was four. Daddy had a stroke in January. Sis says I'm a shiftless no-good and put me in the orphan's home in St. Louis. I bolted last night."

"Damn! Ya walked eighteen, twenty miles in one night? How?"

"Followed the railroad."

"That's a helluva hike for a man, much less a boy. No wonder you're drug out. Sleep any?" He lights a cigarette.

"Yes, sir. In an oak tree."

He laughs. "That a fact? A tree? Won't ya fall out?"

"No, sir. Belt myself to a limb." I'm talking too much.

"Where ya headed?"

"Daddy's. In Kansas. Parsons, I think."

"Ya think? Hell, Stan, er, Frankie, Kansas is a big state. Ya better know where yer goin' or ya'll wander 'round lost like them Jews in the Bible, causin' trouble."

"A railroad town. Parsons. Pretty sure."

He sticks out his hand. "Name's Paul. Can't do more fer ya in the way of grub nor money, with payday a week off and mouths to feed. But I know where ya can clean up. Mebbe get new duds. Then, I'll carry ya to Chester. That'll put ya forty-five miles closer to Kansas."

We drive to the farm of two widowed sisters. "Customers," Paul says. "They'll plant hybrid corn come Spring."

The ladies don't ask questions, they just run water in a tub. The tall, skinny one dips a rag in kerosene. "This takes off creosote, but it stings." When the tub's filled, she hands me a cake of Lifebuoy. "Scrub hard, boy."

When I've dried off, the black-haired sister with the thick glasses brings me a shirt and pair of pants. "Yers are ruint." She kinda smiles. "Had a boy oncet. Went to war when he was eighteen. Never come home. Clothes were his'n when he were yer age."

In the car, scrubbed clean of creosote, my belly full of bacon and eggs, I sleep.

12

BUNT

Paul shakes me awake. "This is Chester's city park. Highway's two blocks south." He hands me a stick of Juicy Fruit and squeezes my hand. "Good luck. Hope ya find yer daddy." He drives off with a wave of his hand.

I sit on a park bench listening to crows quarrel in the tall elms above me. I'm on my own. Again. Miles from Kansas, I reckon. Broke. Hungry. The story of my life the last few days. When the sugar's gone from my gum, I head for the highway.

A sign reads, "Cape Girardeau, 119 miles." That'll take me, what, five, six days? With no food, or money. *Walker*, I think, *you got yourself into a pickle.*

My legs won't do the walk-then-run thing like last night, so I trudge in the grass and weeds beside the road. When I get to Kansas, I'll play baseball every day. Saturday nights me and Daddy'll go foxhunting with our new dogs. Before we hit the woods, I'll bait up on beans and ham hock that Daddy'll cook. And cornbread. We'll chase our hounds running Ol' Red all night like always. But right now I'd gladly put up with Sis's lecture on cooperation if she had Chef Boyardee heating on her hotplate.

The trees, the grass, even the sky seems gray. My eyes feel scratchy. My head aches. I want to cry. A stand of elms touches the sky. They're easy to climb with strong sturdy limbs and not much sway. I pick out a tall, slender tree, jump high, and pull myself into the bough, hard work with my weak legs. I belt myself to a limb and fall asleep while gnats buzz my ears, tree bark gouges my legs, crickets chirp, and white clouds sail a blue sky.

❧

A warm sun brings me awake. From up high, a creek glimmers behind those tall sycamore trees. My gut growls. I'm so hungry, I'm weak. I drop to the ground and follow a fisherman's path beneath hickory and ash trees beside tea-colored water.

Sure wish I had a plate of Daddy's Spam and eggs. Or a bowl of Pep cereal to suck down while Sis yammers that my rent is due Saturday and it's only Sunday. The creek looks inviting. A quick dip will wake me up, make me think better.

A weeping willow bends over a wide water hole. I hang my overalls and shirt on a bush and ease into creek water. Last summer Daddy taught me to dog paddle. I promised him I'd never swim alone, so I sit chest-high in the cool water watching bugs skim the smooth surface. I need food. Some folks catch catfish with their bare hands in deep holes, but if I snagged one how would I cook it with no fire, frying pan, or grease?

I spy a blackberry vine growing just off the path. I wade buck naked in among briars and stickers, stuffing the small, sour berries into my mouth as fast as I can. It doesn't take long to gobble what berries I can find, and my gut still growls.

Back in the water, I remember I've got thirty cents in my pocket. What will that buy? I'll need a dollar, maybe five, to get to Kansas. I need a plan.

PART III

I use my single windup, my double windup, my triple windup. My hesitation windup, my no windup. I also use my step-'n' pitch, my submariner, my side-armer, and my bat dodger. Man's gotta do what a man's gotta do.

—Satchel Paige, Legendary Black League Pitcher, member Baseball's Hall of Fame.

13

Double Header

I hear water splashing. Probably muskrats. I duck behind a willow to look. It's not a muskrat, but a girl standing neck deep in the creek. She forms an arrowhead with her hands, then dives into the brown water. Her bubbles head straight toward me. Seconds later, she steps up on the creek bank, an arm's length from me. Eyes closed, she pulls a towel from a tree branch and dries her cocoa-colored skin.

Her black eyes pop open. She smells like toothpaste. A bare brown foot almost touches mine. Her mouth forms a circle when she sees me, pulling the towel over her chest. I know a gentleman would look away, but her birthday suit paralyzes me.

I stammer, "Beg...beg your...your pardon, ma'am." Finally, I turn away.

"Where'd you come from?" She doesn't sound mad.

"I, I, I, just...cooled off."

I watch a mud dauber load up on dirt near a puddle of water, then zigzag off. A butterfly tastes a black-eyed Susan swaying in the breeze. A bobwhite quail calls from the brush. The girl says, "You can look now."

She wears a yellow blouse, brown shorts, white tennis shoes. She's short for a full-grown woman, which I can testify she is. She's maybe Sis's age.

She smiles. "Swim or get dressed. White boys with a pecker the size of a clothespin aren't my type."

I run for my clothes.

My hands shake so it's hard to button my shirt. When I'm dressed, the girl sits on a log in the shade, a smile on her red lips. She has small white teeth. Her throat looks smooth as a newborn colt's. Her hair, short. Black. Curly. I wish my pants legs weren't rolled up so high.

"What's the deal, Clothespin?"

"Name's Frankie."

"Okay, Frankie. The truth. Don't tell me you're mushroom hunting or stalking pileated woodpeckers. You're sunburned and frazzled. What are you running from?"

I spill my guts, adding, "I'm headed to Kansas to be with Daddy."

"Quite a story, Frankie Clothespin. It's good you left the orphanage. They ruin kids. You're a far piece from Kansas, though. How'd you get here?"

"Caught a ride with a hybrid-seed corn salesman."

She points to my ball glove. "What position?"

"Shortstop. Centerfield. Pitcher."

"Skill positions, huh?"

I nod. *How would a girl know that?*

"You hungry, Frankie?"

"Yes, ma'am."

"Let's see what I can scrape up. Name's Linda. I play a little ball myself."

Is she the girl pitcher the handbill advertised? Mr. Black Baseball Expert said the barnstorming Black team's pitcher did their cooking.

In the clearing is the biggest car I've ever seen. Purple as mulberry jam, with whitewall tires and gold bumpers. Is this the Heavenly Chariot preachers talk about in church? Is this the purple car the colored ball team travels in, like my friend Paul talked about?

Packard is written in silver letters on the hood. On the door, in red lettering, outlined in gold: *Kansas City River Kings and Mississippi Mud Dogs All-Star Baseball Club, International. Buell Sanders, Manager & Proprietor*

For the first time since my last time at bat, I smile. I did good. Real good.

14

SQUEEZE BUNT/SUICIDE BUNT

I do what chores Linda lets me do and listen as she talks. This is her third year with the Kings. "Every fall I say this is my last year, but when the snow melts and the only cure for the ache in my arm is to throw baseballs, I sign on for another year. Besides, where does a Black girl with little education, modest bookkeeping and cooking skills, but who throws a ball better than most men, Black or white, find a job that pays sixty, seventy bucks a week? Or did, before Mr. Jackie Robinson signed with the Dodgers."

She lowers her voice. "A man's comfort house is not in my game plan. Maybe I'll take up nursing."

I wash the dishes while she dries them—so the callouses on her pitching hand don't go soft. We haven't gone a mile, so on the second day, I say, "I'd get to Kansas faster if I hitchhiked. I want to get there so Daddy and I can foxhunt."

Linda's black eyes flash. "Patience, my friend. With us, you at least eat regular. Plus, you're not out one red cent as long as you do a few chores. You fell into a good deal and aren't smart enough to know it."

I remember the chicken-fried steak she served at supper last night and nod. She's right. I'm busted as a wind-blown limb. Still, I want to see Daddy and hear our hounds top a ridge, hot on a fox's trail.

Linda says, "We'll move tomorrow. Tell you what. Our last two games of the season are in Pittsburg, Kansas. That's spitting distance from Parsons. Stick with us. After the game, I'll drive you there on my way to Omaha."

She smiles. "I don't want to ruin your dream, Frankie, but your daddy may not be like you remember him." She touches my arm. "My auntie had a stroke. A couple of weeks later she took to her bed and stayed there till she died."

I shake my head in disgust. "Not Daddy. He's strong. He was in the hospital only four days. He has a hard time talking, and drags his right foot when he walks, but he was doing better when my sisters moved him to Kansas."

"I hope for your sake he's great. All I'm saying is maybe tamp your dreams down a bit. Didn't you say your oldest sister has four kids? Another mouth to feed might not be welcome."

I've already thought of that. "Me and Daddy won't stay in Kansas. I'll bring him back home so we can hunt in the woods we know, and I'll be close to school like before."

Linda smiles. "That's a nice thought. Do you have the bucks to pull that off?"

I don't answer. I have a lousy thirty cents in my pocket. That's all.

15

PITCHING

The Kings camp out in a pasture outside Joplin, Missouri, on a Thursday morning, getting ready to play the Joplin Merchants Saturday and Sunday. Late Friday afternoon I get a big surprise. The team gathers at the Packard, all wearing their purple and gold uniforms. I later learn that second baseman Jacob Hastings and their leading hitter, Bob Thorpe, drew the short straw, and will stay back to guard the camp.

Graham Glass, the Kings' utility player, gets behind the wheel and drives the Packard in zigzags back and forth across the road, the siren crying like a lost baby. The rest of the team, swinging bats or tossing balls back and forth, march along behind him.

As we come into town, Glass says into the loudspeaker, "Baseball. Baseball. Come see America's number-one traveling team play your local heroes. Free pitching demonstration tonight by Little Linda Lou, baseball's only professional female pitcher."

White boys on bikes and barefoot colored boys join in behind the King ballplayers, waving balloons and giving out Indian war whoops. The Kings' right fielder, Merc McBride, tall and rangy, his face painted white, a purple crown on his head, wearing floppy shoes four feet long, does handstands and gives blown-up balloons to anybody who'll take one.

The Kings even have a band. Base-stealer Sudden Sam plays harmonica, relief pitcher Brice Hamm toots a saxophone, Home Run King Gates blows what he calls the 'bone, and right fielder Bert Bower beats a drum. They step lively, playing tunes like "It's a Hot Time in the Old Town Tonight" and "Take Me Out to The Ballgame."

We parade down Main Street, swing past the First Baptist Church, and march down Thirty-Second Street in front of big white houses with green lawns to South Main and follow it to where the sidewalk ends. The Negro ball diamond sits in a pasture with a pond in deep center field. Town folks follow along, the band serenading them with Sousa marches and jazz tunes. Folks dance and sing, yell at the players, shake hands with neighbors, laugh, and have a good time. When the crowd is shoulder to shoulder, Linda jumps from the Packard.

She wears a purple ball cap with a gold K on the front, her gold earrings gleaming in the late afternoon sun. Her gold uniform top has a big red-and-purple number one on it. Her purple shorts have a red stripe down each side. She wears gold-colored spikes. With her brown skin and black hair, she's a pretty sight.

Linda waves and bows, juggling four baseballs all the while. "Here she is," Graham Glass announces. "Little Linda Lou. America's only professional female pitcher. Test your skills. Get a hit off her and win big money."

16

DOCTORING THE BASEBALL

In her free pitching exhibitions, Linda wows the crowd with her pitching skills. Her first trick is to put three bottles on home plate, then she goes to the mound, winds, and throws a curveball that bends in between bottles one and three and sends the middle bottle flying. This is hard to do once, but when onlookers bet that she can't do it again, she does it four more times.

Someday I hope to throw a curve as wicked as hers. But nobody will ever be as pretty as Linda when she throws a baseball. Her snapping black eyes, tan skin, red lips, and white teeth make her more than beautiful. Still, the real fun starts when men bet cash money that they can hit her pitching.

Pops Buell places a big jar stuffed with dollar bills next to home plate. Graham Glass stirs up the crowd by announcing, "Step right up. Rap a hit. Win big money. A round quarter gets you five square swings."

Pops hands a bat to a boy in a ball cap. "Here. Give it a rip. Free."

Linda tosses him a fat pitch even Sis could hit. The boy sends a weak grounder to left field since there are no fielders on the diamond. Glass says, "See? If he'd fed the jar, he could take his girl out for a hamburger and a movin' picture show and still buy his momma red roses."

Two or three men drop quarters—one a dollar—in the jar. Linda puts juice on the ball now. The batters swing and miss from here to Sunday. To juice things up, Delray, the Kings regular center fielder, who's white as I am, steps up, swinging a bat. He's disguised in a floppy hat, a red wig, thick-rimmed eyeglasses, blue work shirt, and overalls. He lays five bucks on home plate.

"Let's see what ya got, girl."

Linda pitches and Delray drives three straight pitches into the outfield, one over the fence. "If an old man with glasses can hit her, you young boys can too."

He hands the bat to a young man wearing a St. Louis Browns ball cap and lays another fiver on home plate. "Five bucks says he hits."

Buell yells, "You're faded. Anyone else?"

The batter is a star on the local team, so six or seven supporters lay dollar bills next to Buell's money. Linda throws a flat curve. The hitter lines it to left field. His backers clap and yell. "That's the way! That Black girl is no match for you."

On the microphone, Glass says, "Little Linda, you got yourself a hitter."

The winners stuff Buell's money in their pockets, strut like banty roosters and slap backs. Buell lays out five more singles. Onlookers, sure their heroes can hit this girl pitcher, plunk down folding money. Linda fires five pitches not even the great Joe DiMaggio could hit. The batters swing and miss. Buell lets his winnings stay on home plate, like the money's not important.

"Who else wants to give it a go?"

The town team players the Kings will play tomorrow plunk down their money, grab their bats, and step up to the plate. To build the pot, Linda feeds them easy pitches at first. They foul some off her tosses or hit weak ground balls that roll out to where a shortstop would normally play. When the pot builds, Linda's curves swerve and her fastballs sizzle. One guy who put up five dollars swings ten times without hitting so much as a foul ball. He throws his bat in the dirt and glares out at Linda.

"They's Mexican jumpin' beans in them balls. A real ball don't hop 'round like that. Not even Haz could hit them."

"Who's Haz?" Delray asks.

"Jake Hazlett. Played for the Columbus Redbirds. Hurt his arm, so he's home until he can throw. He hits like Musial." That I doubt. No one hits like Musial, except Musial. I don't say this out loud, only think it.

The guy who's sure the balls contain jumping beans, says,

"Haz is our first baseman, now. He'll hit this girl like he's smashin' walnuts when he gets here."

About that time a car grinds to a stop behind the bleachers. A young man carrying a bat walks fast toward home plate. A fan yells, "Here's Jake! Show this gal she ain't got shit."

Delray shakes Jake's hand. "Glad to meet ya, Mr. Hazlett. Heard lots about you." He turns to Pops Buell. "Your gal's in trouble now."

"Ya better believe it," Haz says. He has strong-looking arms and shoulders. He wears a red-and-blue Cardinals ball cap, a white sweatshirt with red sleeves, and white uniform pants. He has on slippers, his baseball spikes slung over his shoulder.

To Little Linda, Delray says, "Your goose is cooked, girl. This gentleman led all of Double-A baseball in home runs last year."

Buell comes up, a big smile on his face. "Pleased to meet ya, Mr. Hazlett. Ya sure ya wanna waste time hittin' my girl pitcher?"

"Tryin' to chicken out, huh," Hazlett says. "Just like a darkie."

Buell ignores this. "Ya want a practice swing or two?"

"Nah. I can hit anything a girl throws," he says, and adds, "in my PJs and with my eyes closed." The crowd cheers when they hear this.

"Good," Buell says. "One quarter buys ya five swings. No bunts allowed. Hit two fair, ya win the pot." Buell lays another dollar on home plate. "Here's my money. Where's yers?"

The crowd murmurs. A tall man in a blue suit, white shirt, and blue-and-yellow tie trots toward home plate. "The mayor," a fan says.

"Wait a minute. Wait a minute," he yells. "Jake Hazlett's a professional. He don't play for pennies." It's the mayor who's talking. "Let's make it interestin'. Let's say if he hits yer pitcher twicet in five throws ya pay him fifty bucks. I got fifty bucks says he can do that. That too rich for ya?"

"Maybe we can scrape up 'nuff to cover it," Buell says, peeling off five ten-dollar bills.

The mayor smiles like a rodeo clown and pulls a fifty from his billfold. He smooths it out and lays it next to Buell's money. Buell says, "I got a ballplayer down each line to call fair or foul. Ya trust 'em, or want yer own?" The mayor nods to two townspeople who trot out behind first and third. Buell calls to Linda. "Ya got a hitter, girl. Show 'em whatcha got."

In the batter's box, Jake Hazlett takes a practice swing and digs his spikes into the dirt. He probably uses a Louisville Slugger bat. He nods at Linda. She winds and fires a fastball, low and away. Jake swings and misses. The crowd groans.

Linda pitches again. Fastball. Jake sizzles a frozen rope over second base. "That's the way," a fan yells. The crowd applauds. Hazlett has three more swings to get one hit and win the hundred-dollar pot, plus Buell's fifty.

Linda winds and throws like usual. The ball speeds toward home plate. As Jake starts his swing, the ball seems to stop, like a yoyo on a string. The truth is, Linda's arm speed is the same as it was on the fastball Hazlett creamed, but this time she gripped the ball a different way, so the ball moves at a different speed—her change of pace. Hazlett swings, misses, and almost falls onto the dirt. The ball slaps harmlessly into Taveras's mitt.

The crowd shuffles their feet and groans. This is not what they want. Their hero is supposed to smash this Black girl's every pitch from here to New Orleans. Now he has two swings left to get one hit.

Jake shouts, "Throw that again and I'll hit it five miles."

I'd like to laugh, but when I yelled and clapped at the last pitch, Merc McBride, still wearing the purple crown he wore in the parade, gave me a hard look. So I bite my tongue and smile. When Jake nods he's ready, Linda fires a curveball, inside and low. Jake swings and sends it down the left field line. Foul by fifty feet.

The crowd goes quiet as midnight in the woods now. Their hero has one pitch left. He doesn't have to hit the ball long or far. Just fair. Left field, center, or right. Anywhere. "C'mon, Jake, get serious," a fan yells.

17

DOUBLE OR NOTHING

Night's coming on and the way Jake lollygags he probably hopes the contest will be called for darkness. He dusts his bat with resin, knocks dirt from his spikes, adjusts his uniform pants, wipes his hands, takes a bunch of practice swings, adjusts his pant legs again. Finally, he nods at Linda. She starts her windup. Jake steps out of the box.

He's trying to get her mad, but Linda only smiles and waits until Jake nods, then fires. The pitch looks like a fastball. Jake strides and swings, ready to knock that ball a mile. Then, just as the bat is about to meet the ball, it swerves down and away. Linda's drop ball. Jake's bat hits only air. Linda wins the pot.

The crowd boos. "Damn it, Haz, you let a girl beat ya. A Black one to boot."

Buell stoops to pocket his winnings. Mr. Mayor runs up.

"Not so fast. Not so fast. I'll be a gentleman and give ya darkies a second chance. Let's go double or nothin'. Ya good fer that?"

Buell says, "I don't know. That's a steep hill for us poor coloreds. We're here to play ball, not gamble."

I wonder, Will Buell walk away with the money he's won so far? There's another half hour of good light. Why not use it?

Buell says, "A hundred bucks is a big chunk for us ballplayers."

"It were yer brag," says Mr. Mayor. "Ya dance, ya gotta pay the fiddler. Ya claimed yer girl was so good my man couldn't hit two fair balls outta five pitches. Now that he's warmed up, ya gonna chicken out? Can't yer players pony up a sawbuck or two if she's so good? After all, they's professionals."

Buell studies his shoes. "I reckon maybe I can scrape up a hundred. Small bills okay?"

"Whatever. Long as it spends."

Buell takes two or three steps and turns. "How 'bout this? Let's do two bets. A hundred fer the team. Double or nothin'. An' a side bet 'tween us gentlemen. Say, 'nother fifty? Double or nothin'."

The mayor smiles big. "It's yer money. I can cover however much ya wanna lose."

Mr. Mayor lays two fifties next to Buell's five twenties, then pulls another hundred dollars from his wallet. He smooths the bills carefully and lays them across Buell's pile. "You're faded, barnstormer."

The mayor's certain sure, now that Jake's seen Linda pitch, he has her pitches figured out. After all, she's a girl, and Jake Hazlett hit more home runs than anyone else in all of Double-A baseball last year. No way she can handle a professional like Haz.

All eyes are on Jake. He takes maybe a dozen practice swings, steps up to the plate, taps his bat on it and digs his spikes into the dirt. Taveras crouches behind him, his big mitt Linda's target. "You and me, lady, you and me," he says.

Jake nods. Linda winds and fires. Hazlett swings. Hickory bat meets horse-hide ball. The ball climbs into the sky, soaring high and deep, landing far beyond the outfield fence. A long home run.

The crowd roars. Mr. Mayor calls, "That's showin' her, Haz! She'll think twice about messin' with a white boy."

Hazlett smiles big. He's probably thinking, *I've got her number now. Two more good swings and that hundred-dollar pot is mine. Ready to pay up, girl?*

If I could, I'd tell Linda to throw him low and away. She told me her fastball swerves down as it reaches the plate. *That would fool Haz, I'm thinking.* Linda kicks dirt, disgusted that she threw him the fastball he wanted and expected. "Fast-ball hunting," they call it.

I bet Linda says to herself, "Get in the game, girl. One more hit and you go home. Broke."

"Ah right, girlie," Mr. Mayor yells. "Yer tits are in the ringer now. How ya gonna get 'em loose?" The crowd laughs.

18

CHANGE OF PACE

Linda nods to Jake Hazlett that she's ready to pitch, toes the rubber, winds, and fires. The ball comes in letter high. Hazlett strides and swings, but as his bat is about to send the ball flying, it swerves inside as good four-seam fastballs do. Jake's bat whiffs air.

"Throw that lollypop agin, and I'll knock the cover off it," he yells.

Linda told me she can throw seven different pitches for strikes. Now, she rolls the ball in her right hand, goes into her windup and pitches. Maybe two feet from the plate, it sails inside and down. Her sinker. Hazlett swings and hits the ball into the dirt just outside the batter's box. It spins backward and rolls to a stop. Foul ball.

Two pitches left for Jake Hazlett to get one hit.

Hazlett steps out of the box, pulls at his pants, takes a vicious practice swing, steps back into the box, and nods ready to Linda. She takes a deep breath, wiggles her rear end, and fires. Hazlett swings. Hickory bat meets horsehide ball. The ball climbs high into the sky, arching back toward the backstop. A foul ball.

Taveras flips off his catcher's mask. "Lo tengo. Lo tengo. I got it! I got it!" The ball settles into his mitt. One pitch left for Hazlett to get one hit, one last chance for Jake Hazlett, the fearsome Double-A home-run hitter to show a Black girl pitcher how a real man hits a baseball. Jake knocks dirt from his cleats, takes another vicious practice swing, and nods.

19

SWINGING STRIKE

Friday afternoon at the Negro ballpark, it's what Daddy would call nut-cutting time. If Hazlett hits a fair ball, he wins the $200 Winner-Take-All pot. If he hits a foul ball or swings and misses, Little Linda pockets the money. Hazlett knows this. Linda knows this. The crowd knows this. Buell knows this. And for sure the red-faced, sweating town mayor knows this. The crowd's quiet as a cemetery at midnight as their hero, Jake Hazlett, stands in the batter's box hoping he can get that hit.

Hazlett takes a practice swing and nods. Linda pitches. The ball speeds toward home plate with the spin and speed of a fastball. Hazlett swings, hoping to give that horsehide a long ride. Then, in the half second before bat meets ball, it seems to stop. Again. Linda's change of pace. Again.

Hazlett jerks his bat back, loses his balance, and falls into the dirt as the ball smacks sweetly into Traveras's big mitt. In a real game, the ump would jerk his thumb in the air and yell, "Steerike three. Yer out."

But this is not real baseball. This is a contest between a white minor-league ballplayer trying to put a Black girl pitcher in her place, sending her home broke, with his pocket filled with money, while a mostly white hometown crowd looks on, cheering his every move. Baseball rules are gone now.

In a real game, if the ump didn't call that "Strike three," I'd yell, "Get in the game, Blue." So would other players, even if you know the ump won't change his mind. I'm sure Pops Buell knows his argument won't change a thing either, but after playing many a ball game over many a summer in small-town ballparks before hometown fans and in large stadiums in New York City, Patterson, New Jersey, and Kansas City, Missouri.

Playing against white professional ballplayers and Negro teams with Standing Room Only signs flashing, the habit to protect your player at all costs takes over. He runs onto the field. "Yer man's out. He swung and missed. Game's over."

"Horseshit," Mr. Mayor says, kicking up dirt with his black dress shoes. "That pitch was a foot outside. Ain't a umpire alive who'd call it a strike, and we ain't got no ump. Tell yer gal to throw a pitch my man can reach with a bat, not a telephone pole. She does, he'll hit it a mile."

Buell throws his hands up. "Yer man went around. He's out."

"He don't havta swing at ever'thing yer gal throws. He don't havta go after the ball. Yer pitcher's afraid to throw a strike 'cause my guy will bust it. You might cheat others but not me and Haz. This ain't battin' practice. This is for money."

At home plate, Hazlett brushes dirt from his knees and looks to the sky, like maybe God will show mercy on him and he'll hit one of Linda's pitches after all. The way he acts, the smirk on his face, says he knows he swung, but he'll admit that only after they pull the third tooth from his tender gums with a pair of needle-nose pliers. He points his bat at Linda. "Throw a strike and I'll bust it."

Buell knows when to retreat. He turns and trots to his usual place near first base. "Okay, girl. You got him, so put him away now."

Mr. Mayor, puffed up like a bantam rooster, claps his hands. "Bust her, Haz. Bust her, boy."

Traveras tosses the baseball back to Linda. She catches it with a snap of her glove. Taveras moves in front of the plate and slaps his mitt with a big fist. "You and me, lady. You and me."

Linda flips the ball from hand to hand, then pops it in her glove. Traveras squats. Hazlett nods ready. Linda wiggles her rear end, raises her arms, kicks her left leg high, brings her right arm back and then forward. The ball speeds toward home plate.

It looks like a fastball, middle in, thigh high, what ballplayers call his wheelhouse, just where he wants it. He's sure Linda won't dare to throw him three straight changeups, so his strong arms send the bat through the air in a wicked arc, aiming to send that ball on a long ride into the silver air of the evening. Then, as it did before, the ball seems to die. Hazlett tries to stop his bat, but it's too late. His swing twists his legs and hips. He falls in a heap in the dust of the batter's box. The ball pops untouched into Traveras's mitt.

Little Linda, America's only professional female pitcher, has just struck out Jake Hazlett, Double-A Baseball Home Run King. She wins four hundred greenback dollars in the player's pot and another two hundred smackeroos from the mayor. I jump to my feet and yell, ignoring Merc McBride's stern look.

"I'll get even with ya Black bastards," the mayor screams, spit spraying from his lips. His face red, his dress shirt wet with sweat, he throws his hat down, kicks it, and turns to face Buell, his fist pulled back like he's going to slug him. The mayor realizes Buell would wipe him up like a dish rag. He screams, "She didn't throw one fuckin' strike the whole time. Nobody can hit what they can't reach."

Buell ignores this and stuffs the money into his pockets. "Me and my boys, especially our pitcher, 'preciate the opportunity to play a little ball with ya, mayor. Had lots of fun."

"Shut the fuck up, asshole."

At home plate, Hazlett, still on his knees, his face pale, his jersey wet with sweat, beats his bat against home plate. "I shoulda killed her. She ain't got nothin'."

Buell heads to the Packard at a fast clip, waving to the players. "Hustle up, fellas. Let's get out while we can."

The ballplayers pile into the Packard, leaving a place for Linda. She pulls me in next to her. Some players hop onto running boards, holding on to the straps used to buckle down tents and baseball equipment so they won't fall. Glass drives fast through town, the car bouncing over bumps and railroad tracks, the ballplayers laughing and yelling, having a grand old time.

20

Pay Off

In Linda's tent, Buell hands Oscar Traveras and Graham Glass each a ten-spot. He says to Little Linda, "Here's twenty-five from the team's hundred. And twenty from my bet with the mayor." He smiles. "We was up eighty-one bucks 'fore the mayor showed up. Here's another fifteen."

Linda takes the money but doesn't smile. "How about another twenty? I've expenses too, you know."

"I'm bein' more 'n fair. In barnstormin' we share the rewards and the expenses." He goes to the tent flap. "I'll go pick up Ruby, then come pay my ballplayers. Okay?"

I help Linda put out cold cuts with all the trimmings, while the players clean up. Most make ham or baloney sandwiches, swallow deviled eggs, and stand outside Linda's tent. They've showered, shaved, and dressed for the occasion. Some wear blue velvet, black satin, even red leather pants and yellow or green silk shirts with orange or purple suspenders. Some don red shoes. Some green. Glass wears pointy-toed orange ones with metal around the heel and toe. Most guys favor hats. Cream-colored, or yellow with wide brims. Merc McBride and Jacob Hastings wear blue hats with narrow brims they call fedoras. The smell of rose water, lilac, and Ivory soap is strong.

Glass says, "Ya dress good, look good, smell good, and flash a wad of twenties, you just might get lucky." Everyone laughs.

Bob Thorpe, the Kings' fine third baseman and leading hitter, stammers, "Is, is, is that 'fore, 'fore the la—lady sees the twen—twenties or af—after?" The guys roar at this.

Glass grins. "Ain't nothin' sweeter than a pretty country girl tryin' to earn her way to the big city. They'll get on their knees and make promises, then make good on the promise." This draws a big laugh.

Buell parks his Packard and comes up, slapping backs, shaking hands, like the players are long-lost family he hasn't seen for years. "Good to see ya, ballplayer. How ya been?" Ruby watches, quiet as a bobcat in a tree. Buell pulls a wad of cash from his pocket and counts out every dollar owed each player, giving each one the paper Linda wrote up that shows their expenses and final earnings.

They say, "Thanks, Pops. Thank ya mightily. A pleasure playin' baseball for you. Thanks for payin' me money to play for ya."

Buell's gold teeth shine. "We got us a good team. 'Member you're my ambassador tonight. Leave them white girls alone. No fights, okay. Leave yer knifes, razors, and guns in yer tent, hear?" He throws each a gold package.

"Put a blanket on your stallion. Nothin' ruins a team like The Drip. Have a good time and sell a ticket or two."

21

GREEN LIGHT

Linda was counting on Buell to bring her breakfast fixings—
eggs, bacon, flour—for Saturday morning. He says, "Sorry, girl.
Me and Ruby are workin' on a problem pertainin' to the team's
well-bein' and didn't have time to shop."

Ruby nods. "For sure, for sure, Miss Linda."

Buell says, "I'll drop you off at the store in Saginaw." That's
a small town down the road a piece. "Use petty cash. Take the
white boy along for company. You can walk home. Nice evenin'
for a stroll."

Linda frowns. "I'd feel more comfortable if you'd drive me."

"Normally, I would. But tonight I've bidness to handle back
at the hotel."

Ruby touches Linda's arm. "He's right. We're on the clock to
get back to the hotel. Sorry, dear."

Linda shrugs and turns to me. "Okay, Frankie Clothespin.
It's you and me."

It's almost dark when Linda and I climb out of the Packard in
front of a store with a sign that reads *Groceries Standard Oil Beer.*
A feed store is next door. The tavern's neon sign across the
street blinks *Beer, Beer, Beer.* Three or four dusty pickup trucks
are parked on the street. You can hear the jukebox, loud talk,
and laughter. Two white houses under tall maple trees are the
only other buildings in town.

Linda says, "Here's a ten, Frankie. You go in. My going in
might not be wise." She moves into the shadows, glancing at the
tavern. It's not cold, but I see her shiver.

"Get five dozen eggs. Three pounds of bacon. Sack of

flour. No candy. No ice cream. No soda pop. Just what I said. And hurry."

Inside, Mr. Storekeeper looks up from his wrinkled newspaper, but stays seated. He must figure I'm looking to buy penny candy. When I lay the ten on the counter, he rushes up, smiling. "What can I do for ya, young man?"

I repeat Linda's list. Mr. Storekeeper sacks up my order. "Ya ain't from 'round here, are ya?"

"Sure am. Born and raised. Back for a visit. I'm Mick Walker's oldest boy, Franklin. Remember Daddy? Taught high school in Joplin?"

The storekeep takes off his glasses and looks me up and down. "Why, sure. Now that I look close, I see you're his spitting image. How's he doing? Still teachin'?"

"No, sir. He's principal now. Makes a ton more money. Momma had twin girls last January. Daddy says the corn he planted down by the creek will yield fifty bushels an acre come harvest time. He's smart. Planted hybrid." If you're going to lie, make it a big one.

"That gal with you? She local?"

"No, sir. Jeff City. Rich as Rockefeller. Her daddy's the governor of the State of Missouri."

I'm out the door before Mr. Storekeeper can ask more questions. Linda comes from the shadows and takes a sack. We walk fast for fifty yards before she speaks. "Buell's got money problems. That's why he bet like he did tonight. To make payroll. He probably wired his bank for an advance on tomorrow's ticket sales, but the money won't arrive till later. That's why he had to get back to his hotel tonight, why we have to walk."

A green pickup truck that was parked in front of the tavern drives past and honks. I wave.

Linda says, "Stop that! Act like you don't see or hear a thing. Just walk."

I'm taken aback. I figure the driver's a baseball fan who probably wants tickets to the game. I don't understand why she's so mad.

The truck turns around, whips past us, then slows so we have to just mosey, or we'll stumble over it. After maybe forty yards, it zooms off, dust flying, makes a U-turn, and barrels back full speed. We jump into the ditch. The truck screeches to a stop, its bumper maybe five feet away from us. The driver, his body half out of the window, yells, "Hey, good lookin'. Want a ride? I need me some brown sugar."

Now I see that's he's white. Skinny. Adam's apple big as a baseball. Daddy would say, "If we had his nose full of nickels, we'd have rent money fer a year."

Linda whispers, "Don't talk. Walk."

A gob of tobacco juice just misses my foot. "This yer boy, sugar?"

The pickup roars off again, turns around and races back at us, horn blaring. Two baseball bats away, it skids to a stop. "Get outta the road, animals."

We're walking in the ditch as it is.

Linda whispers, "Ignore him. Just walk."

I wish she'd tell this idiot to get lost.

The road makes a curve around a vacant pasture. Linda ducks under the rusty barbed wire. I follow her. There's no road here, so the pickup can't follow. The grass is knee high, wet with evening dew. It's maybe a half mile from our camp, the tents dark shadows beneath a stand of trees.

Linda squats behind a stand of persimmon sprouts. "I'll hide. Sam and Gates are in their tents. Run and get 'em, Frankie. Fast."

I race through knee-high grass like I'm running out a triple, sticking close to the fence line so Skinny can't see me. I bust into Gates's tent without knocking. He's shining his cleats for tomorrow's game. He listens to my wild rant, pulls on his overalls, and grabs a ball bat.

"Show me the way, boy."

Sudden Sam hears me and comes running, still dressed in Kings purple uniform bottoms. "You two go ahead. I'll catch up."

It's dark now, with a crooked moon and a slight breeze. Skinny's truck idles in the road across from the pasture where Linda crouches behind persimmon trees, with him leaning on the driver's-side door. "Hey, girlie girl. I'm ready for my brown sugar. C'mon now."

He's so interested in Linda he doesn't see us until Gates slams his rear tire with his bat. Startled, Skinny turns toward the noise. Sudden Sam steps from the shadows, something silver in his hands.

"Get in the pickup and go, white man. Or stay and die."

Skinny throws his hands into the air. "Don't shoot. Don't shoot." He slides behind the steering wheel, twists the ignition key, revs the engine and speeds off. Out of pistol range, he stops. "Pull a gun on me, boy. Ya'll pay." Then his taillights disappear into the night.

Linda comes up. She's breathing fast. "You saved my bacon. And yours."

Gates says, "White man lookin' for trouble always finds it."

Sam taps his pistol. "I've got more trouble than he can handle."

"Hope ya don't havta use it, my friend," Gates says. "Linda, go to your tent and stay there. Anyone comes calling, scream. Me and Sam will keep watch out here in case this white man is stupid enough to come back."

Linda says, "Rednecks like him run in packs. He'll be back. When he comes he'll bring a bunch of idiots with him. That's the Klan way."

"Yeah," Sudden Sam says. "And a Black man ends up getting lynched for protecting his place of residence."

22

Brouhaha

Daddy told me about the Ku Klux Klan. One night before I was born, he was foxhunting when he smelled smoke and saw flames over by White Cloud Baptist Church. He thought the church was on fire, so he ran over to help put out the fire. He came up the rise in the road about a half mile from the church and saw a bunch of men in a circle, dressed in sheets, wearing tall pointy hats, and watching a cross burn.

"I'd come up on a Klan ceremony," Daddy said. "If they catch me, I'm a dead man. I ducked into a gully and followed it uphill. At the top, I lit out for home fast as I could run, leavin' dogs in the woods. Spoke nary a word to anyone what I seen, not even your momma. The Klan's bad news, son."

I've traveled with the Kings from Illinois through Missouri. They've won all four ball games played. Last weekend they beat the Cape Girardeau Merchants two games. Saturday and yesterday they put away the Joplin Merchants.

One of the most fun parts about watching the Kings is batting practice before the game. Each player bats twice, taking six swings each time, not counting bunts. A handkerchief lies along the first- and third-base lines. The batter bunts the ball. Each time, the ball rolls to a stop in the middle of that hanky, first down the third-base line, then first. With the bunts done, the batter calls, "Left field," and hits a screaming line drive there. Then center, then right field. Each time the ball goes where he called. After that, it's frozen ropes to the outfield or long bombs out of the ballpark.

Outfield practice ends with each outfielder showing off his

arm. Graham Glass sets a water bucket on second and third base. The fielder catches a fly ball and makes a one-hop throw that bounces into the bucket. Every time. Impressive, but not as amazing as the way infield practice ends.

During infield, Glass hits grounders to each infielder. The shortstop grabs the ball, whips it to the second baseman, who fires to first. The first baseman catches it and throws home. The catcher lets loose a BB to second, which the second baseman gloves and fires to third. The third baseman—Bob Tharp— turns as he catches the ball and makes a perfect strike to the catcher. Each play is smooth, the white ball speeding across the diamond, the pop of leather ball hitting leather glove, the purple uniforms and gold spikes as pretty as a field of ripe wheat when the wind moves across it a row at a time.

Then comes the best part. Glass tosses three balls into the air at the same time. With one swing of the bat he hits a ground ball to all three infielders. The third baseman fields the ball like usual and throws to first. Pops Buell catches it and tosses it high in the air, then gloves the shortstop's throw, flips it in the air, snags the second baseman's toss, and flips it the same way. Then Buell turns and catches the first ball behind his back, wheels and grabs the second ball and the third one, then fires each one at Taveras. He bows then and trots off the field with the other ballplayers at his side.

As Paul, the hybrid-seed corn salesman and Mr. Black Baseball Expert, said back in Illinois, "It ain't baseball but it sure is entertainin'." Paul was also right when he said the Kings keep the score close in the first game so they can sell more tickets for the second game. But on Sunday, they wear their hitting clothes, and usually win big. In the four games I've seen, Suitcase Paine was the Kings' starting pitcher, with Brice Hamm relieving him in the fourth inning Saturday, but on Sunday, Little Linda trots out to the mound instead of Brice.

Graham Glass works the loudspeaker for the Kings. "Now pitching for the Mississippi Mud Dogs and River Kings, Little Linda Lou, baseball's only professional female baseball pitcher.

She better have her stuff today because this local team is a fear-some bunch."

Some in the crowd remember Linda's battle with Jake Hazlett Friday evening. Some boo, while others cheer. As usual, Linda's on her game and the locals don't score a run. The first game she pitched, she allowed only two cheap base hits. One of these came when Delray in center field and the other two outfielders took chairs with them and sat while the home team batted.

A hitter lifts an easy fly ball to center field. Delray pretends to lose it in the sun, and it drops for a hit, and Delray can't find the ball. The batter runs for second. Delray's throw is wild, probably on purpose, so the runner heads for third. Buell, backing up the base, pegs the ball there. The runner sees this and runs back to second, only to see that the second baseman has the ball, so he turns and runs for third. The entire Kings team—outfielders, shortstop, even Linda—chase the poor guy back and forth from second base back to third, then back to second and back to third—a hot box or pickle, it's called. Finally, the runner says, "Tag me. I'm outta steam."

On the loudspeaker, Glass says, "For those keeping score, that's the old eight to three to five to six to seven to one to three, routine play. Any way you score it, the runner's out. And I do mean out. O. U. T." The crowd laughs at this.

In the game, Pops Buell, his big belly covered by a purple shirt with a red number seven on it, his white hair peeking out from under his purple cap, plays first base. Linda said Buell was a star center fielder for the New York Black Giants in the Negro National League during his younger years. Lightning fast, with a rocket arm, he led the league in home runs for five years. He still swings a mean bat.

"If he was white, he'd have played in the Bigs, maybe made Cooperstown," Linda says.

I know that Cooperstown is a town in New York State where baseball's Hall of Fame is located. "That he's Black kept him from taking even one swing in the majors. Instead, he spent his career playing jerk-water towns like Des Moines and Jeff City and Lincoln, Nebraska. Not in the Bigs with the Yankees or the Red Sox where he belonged. A Hall of Fame career wasted."

I nod. I'm not up on Buell, but I sure love seeing Lloyd Gates, the Home Run King, pulverize a baseball. He hit five long home runs, and I mean long, in the four games. Sudden Sam put on a show too. He stole second and third on the same pitch. Twice. Yesterday he turned a bunt into a triple, then stole home.

At night the team sleeps in two big tents with Suitcase and Sudden Sam in Tent One, first row. Suitcase's arms are as long as a Louisville Slugger, his hands as big as home plate. His thin legs covered by a sheet, he takes the coffee I bring him and slaps my hand.

"Not bad for a white boy. Now get out so I can dress."

He wears a red straw hat with a black feather, cream-colored shirt, creased gray trousers, and shined oxblood shoes most every day. He drives a black Cadillac and spends most nights out of camp. When he does sleep in the tent, he's up and out by ten-thirty or eleven, returning around four o'clock every day for practice.

He's serious about playing ball. During batting practice he runs from home plate to second base fast, like he's legging out a double. Then he leads off a few steps and when the pitcher throws to the batter, Suitcase dashes for third, rounds the base, and sprints home. He does this maybe ten times, then he goes to play long toss, where two guys throw high flies to each other. After fifteen or twenty minutes of long toss, he takes to the mound and fires fastballs and curves till Taveras says, "Had 'nuff? My hand's gonna swell."

Suitcase says, "I do the same routine every time. Every day. Haven't had a sore arm or missed one game in my career, soon to be twenty-one years."

Before he quits for the day, Suitcase and Taveras talk over which pitches he'll throw in the game. Then he climbs into his Caddy and glides off to his hotel room.

Linda says, "Young white ladies like his company. And he theirs."

23

SPEED

Sudden Sam hardly ever speaks and rarely smiles. When I bring him his morning coffee he sets it on a small table next to his bed, swings his small feet to the floor, his legs long and lean, and pulls a pint of whiskey from a bag and steps outside.

"My eye opener," he says.

Linda says this is Sam's only drink of the day. After breakfast has settled, he does pushups and jumping jacks and runs wind sprints until he's covered in sweat. He dries off, using a big red towel, then does sit-ups and leg lifts and squat thrusts. His workout over, he showers, dresses in gray shirt and blue trousers, takes a thermos of coffee or jar of buttermilk to his tent, sits in a straight-back chair with pillows under him, and reads thick books with titles like *The Southern Mind*, *American Dilemma*, and *Birth of a Nation*.

From time to time as he studies, Sam writes in a small red notebook he keeps handy. Before supper he showers again and changes into gray slacks, a white shirt, and black shoes shined to a high gleam. When the other players come to the table, Sam will hand them magazines saying, "Interesting article on page twelve about school integration, and why 'separate but equal' is a farce. I'd like your opinion after you've read it."

Once he said, "More Black folks were lynched in 1946 than any other year. Hell, we fought a war to stop racial injustice but Isaac Woodard, an army sergeant, had his eyes gouged out by a Georgia deputy sheriff, with Woodard in full uniform, mind you—all because he asked a Greyhound bus driver if he could get off the bus to take a leak at the next town.

"President Truman formed a Committee on Civil Rights. They're to give him a firsthand report on violence toward

Blacks." He stood up. "You see, there is hope. Lady Freedom may seem far off, her measured steps slow, but if you listen, you can hear her heartbeat and feel her cool breath on the neck of society. Let's rejoice in the glee of it."

The ballplayers clapped and yelled. Sam bowed. "Thank you, men. We shall overcome." He headed for his tent at a slow walk.

Linda says Sam plans to be a college professor when his playing days are over.

Linda's almost as good a cook as she is a pitcher. For breakfast she fries eggs with ham. Biscuits. Gravy. Pancakes, if you want. Dinner might be stew with chunks of tender beef and carrots and onions and potatoes in gravy. Sometimes it's tuna salad sandwiches seasoned with pepper, chopped onions, and mayonnaise, served on fresh-baked bread. Supper, she'll fix fried chicken and mashed potatoes, or ham and slow-cooked green beans with new potatoes and onions. It's all you can eat, every meal.

She uses a small gas stove to cook on. It's sheltered from the wind and rain by a blue tarp. One whiff of her fried potatoes and onions, or sizzling bacon, makes me hungry all over. Her stove folds into a wooden box that goes on the Packard's roof when the team moves to the next town. She sleeps on a cot in her tent, a kerosene lamp shaped like a ballplayer swinging a bat on her desk.

Linda sees to it that broken bats get repaired. When a ballplayer cracks one, she puts it in a basket next to her desk. When she has five or six, she takes them to a local cabinetmaker, who fills the break with glue and sawdust, even taps small nails into the wood where it broke. Ballplayers will sandpaper the bat handle smooth and wrap it with black tape and it's good as new.

When it's time to eat, the ballplayers sit six to a bench at a long pine table. Sometimes, after everyone has had their fill, they'll drink coffee and talk baseball or play gin rummy and talk baseball. Other than Sudden Sam sharing his readings and observations, baseball is about all they talk about.

Most of my chores, like shelling peas, snapping beans, scrubbing pots and pans, sweeping out tents, I do in a quiet way so I can listen to their talk. I learn that a full arm fake stops a runner in his tracks when he's in a hot box; that to bunt successfully, you "catch" the ball with your bat, not poke at it; that with two outs and a 3–2 count on the batter, the runner takes off with the pitch and runs until the umpire calls third out. I like to work near Linda so I can see her smile and hear her soft, sweet voice.

Before Linda makes a pitch, in practice or a game, she squares her shoulders, holding her glove with three fingers inside and one outside, takes a deep breath, wiggles her rear end, kicks her left leg high, and brings her foot down in the same place every time. That's how I'll pitch from now on.

Linda showed me how to hold a fastball. "You're too young to throw curves. Shorten your stride to home plate. Your pitches will stay in the strike zone that way. Form follows function, Frankie. Practice your delivery until you do it without thinking and repeat it the same way every time. Think about where you want the ball to go. If your form's right, it'll go there. Practice, Frankie Clothespin, and you'll be a great pitcher someday."

Another time she said, "Most folks don't know how to root or encourage a player. It's better to say, 'Catch the ball,' rather than, 'Don't drop it.' With a hitter, say, 'Hit it hard.' That's better than, 'Don't strike out.'"

Linda says Pops Buell's wife, Ruby, loves baseball but thinks the demand for barnstorming has ended. She comes to every game, tall and thin as a postage stamp, wearing a red hat covered with red roses and a purple dress with a big red corsage like the ones Sis says turns a lady's head. During the game, Ruby sits beneath a red parasol in a wooden chair on thick red pillows next to the Kings' dugout, sipping lemonade.

Friday evening, before the players are paid, Ruby goes into Linda's tent, picks up her ledger book and runs a long brown finger with red nail polish down each column like she's a grocer adding up a bill. After a minute, she nods at Linda and lays the book back down on the desk.

24

Tools of Ignorance

Saturday, midmorning, I go to the canopy to help Linda lay out what she calls brunch. She's not there. I set out utensils, stack plates, and put glasses next to where the tea jar will be. Linda still doesn't show. Maybe last night's incident gave her a headache.

I'll drop by her tent to see if she needs my help. When I'm ten or fifteen feet away, I see that the tent flap is open, not zipped to keep out bugs the way she likes. I hear glass break and grunts and slaps like there's a wrestling match going on inside. I peek in. Linda is bent backward over her desk, a man's hand covering her mouth.

"I come fer my brown sugar, girlie. Cooperate and it won't hurt a bit." It's Skinny from last night, the guy with the big nose, who Sudden Sam and Gates ran off.

Linda's blouse is ripped showing her white brassiere. Her fingernails dig at Skinny's face.

"I shoulda taken ya last night," Skinny says. "Ya paradin' 'round wantin' what I got."

Air leaves my lungs like the night Daddy and I were chasing our hounds and I crossed a creek and ran full speed into an electric fence. The jolt knocked me down and caused me to pee my pants. It was maybe five minutes before I could speak. That's me now.

Linda sees me and screams, "Frankie! Help!"

Skinny yanks at Linda's top. Her breasts show brown and pink. "That's more like it, girlie." One arm around her waist, Skinny's long hand paws at her. Linda slams her clenched fists into his face. He laughs but he'll have a shiner tomorrow. "I like a wench that fights. Makes it sweeter."

He grabs Linda's hair and pulls her head back, his arm around her neck in what wrestlers call a Half Nelson. He says, "Watch, boy. I'm gonna do yer mammy."

Linda slams her hip against his. They smash into Linda's desk and sprawl to the tent floor, knocking over the basket Linda puts broken bats in, as they bang and clatter across the room. Linda manages to push Skinny away and scrambles to her feet, pulling me in front of her.

"I can take ya easy," Skinny says, standing up. His pants are unzipped. He smells of sweat and whiskey. He pulls out his knife and with a quick twist of his wrist, snaps out a long silver blade. He has a blue tattoo of a sailing ship on his right wrist. Blood oozes from his cheek. He needs a shave.

"Come for my due, girl." He waves his knife. "Drop yer bloomers and get on yer back, or I'll slice yer face open and cut off yer tits."

Linda says, "Never, you son of a bitch."

Skinny laughs. "This is gonna be fun."

He pushes me with a strong hand and puts a bear hug on Linda, holding his knife inches from her right eye. "What'll be? Tits or face?"

I grab a bat from the pile on the floor and swing for the fence, smashing Skinny's spine. His knife skids across the floor. He falls to his knees. I'd like to bash his head in. Instead, I wham him in the ribs. He whimpers like a lost puppy.

"Kill the asshole," Linda says, her voice hoarse. She's breathing hard. Sweat runs down her face. Her breasts gleam in the dim light. I pull off my shirt and hand it to her. Her hands shake like it's a cold winter day, not hot August. She pulls the shirt around her. She hugs me. Then whispers, "Get help."

Sudden Sam and Gates run to Linda's tent. Skinny slumps on a tree stump, head in his hands. "Come to share the Bible with heathens and collect my due. Her bratty kid busted me with a ball bat."

"That's not how the lady sees it," Sudden Sam says. "All

together now, 'Does that flag still fly o'er the land of the free
and the home of the brave?'" He pauses. "Whose freedom do
they mean?"

Gates's hand is on Skinny's shoulder. "Seems ya was so taken
by the word of God ya just passed out. Have a glass of sweet
tea, neighbor?"

"Shut yer fuckin' mouth."

Sam says, "Our freedom-loving neighbor is in no mood
to neighbor. Has a bad back, I reckon." He glances at me but
doesn't say anything. "What a country. White man breaks into
a Black lady's tent to get his due. What's he owed? All together
now." He sings, "'From every mountain side, let freedom ring.'"

Skinny says, "The wench's kid hit me with a ball bat."

Gates says, "Nah. Ya was prayin' so hard the Lord knocked
ya to the ground."

"Her boy hit me," Skinny sobs.

Gates takes Skinny's arm. "She ain't got a kid. If ya mean
this boy here, he's white as the driven snow and ain't big 'nuff
to swing no bat. No siree." He winks at me. "Ya broke into a
lady's private residence to share the Gospel, got overcome with
the Word and took a fall. That's how we see things."

He motions to Sam, who grabs Skinny's other arm. "Since
ya won't share a friendly glass of tea with the neighbors you
prayed for, we won't keep ya from the important stuff ya gotta
handle today. Don't come back, hear?"

They kinda drag him to his truck. "That little Black bastard
broke my back," Skinny keeps saying. He slumps over his steering wheel. After a while, he drives off.

Linda puts on her uniform like all is well. She has a game
to pitch. Lunch is make-your-own sandwiches with bacon, baloney, pimento cheese, lettuce, onions, and other fixings. The
guys don't like salad, so it goes to waste. If they know about
her visitor of last night or this morning, they don't speak of it.

25

PITCHES

I help Linda clean up, then we ride to the ballpark with Delray. After the game, Buell storms into Linda's tent as if the Kings had lost, which didn't happen. "Ya got us in hot water, girl, runnin' around showin' off yer legs, yer lips red as a turkey gobbler's ass in pokeberry time. Wearin' them big gold earrings."

"And who told me to wear an outfit that shows off I'm a girl," Linda asks. "Pops Buell. That's who."

Buell shrugs. "Do ya havta laugh when ya strike a guy out? That gets folks riled up."

"I don't laugh. I just do a fist pump or slap my glove. Besides, wasn't it Pops who told me to act like I was having fun?"

Buell's voice is low. "Damn it, woman. You and yer struttin' around has riled up the Klan. We're in a peck of trouble if they come callin'." He looks at me. "Why'd ya use a bat on that guy, boy?" Then adds, "Yer supposed to be gone, boy."

Linda steps in front of me. "Leave him alone. He saved me from that asshole. We aren't at the border yet. He stays till then. Besides, we need all the help we can get. Don't touch him, hear me?"

"Calm down, missy. Calm down. We've more baseball to play. Can ya pitch a full game tomorrow? That's what yer paid to do, not flounce 'round like a hussy." He pauses. "Suitcase got called up by Cleveland. Brice's wife is sick. He's goin' home."

Buell shakes his white head. "Too bad about Brice's lady, but good news for Suitcase, even if we gotta bear down a little. I'll overlook yer shenanigans. Let's hope the Klan don't come visitin'. Folks in town say money from the harvest has lured white boys outta town."

Linda ignores this. "That's great news about Suitcase. He

deserves a shot in Cleveland." She pauses. "Brice's wife has been poorly for some time. Her last delivery was a hard one. Now she has heart problems."

Linda looks at Buell like a teacher looks at a kid who's late for school. "I can pitch eighteen innings tomorrow if I have to." She takes a big breath. "You know, Pops, I didn't exactly invite that KKK asshole in for a visit. I was updating the ledger and the next thing I know I'm pulled out of my chair and bent over my desk, with that bastard tearing the buttons off my blouse. He'd have gotten what he wanted if Frankie hadn't cold-cocked him."

Buell waves his hand. "I heard all about it. I'm just sayin' we gotta be alert and on guard tonight." He taps his hip pocket where he probably carries a gun. "Now, go feed my ballplayers. What's happened, happened. We won't mention it again. Okay?"

I follow Linda to the tables and help her lay out supper. She doesn't laugh and tease like usual, just puts cold fried chicken and potato salad left over from this morning on the table with a bowl of spaghetti and bread. The ballplayers eat in a hurry, not talking; they just eat and go to their tents.

Linda and I do the dishes. After the trash is burned, I look for a tree closer to Linda's tent to sleep in. If the Klan comes calling, I want to be there to protect her.

A wild rosebush is in bloom not twenty-five yards from my new tree. I pick an armload of blossoms and knock at Linda's tent. "It's Frankie."

"What do you want?" She unzips her door. She's still in her uniform, with no lights on. She takes the roses without a word and buries her nose in them. When she looks up, her cheeks glisten from tears. "Frankie Clothespin, you're my hero."

White roses next to her brown skin in dim light is a treat for my eyes, I tell you.

26

PASSED BALL

I belt myself to a limb in my new tree but can't sleep. High up like this I see lights still burning in buildings not that far away. I still have tickets that Buell gave me earlier. When I sold newspaper subscriptions, a light on late meant a potential customer was still up. Often, they'll be friendlier then, so I shimmy to the ground and walk fast, hoping to get there before they close. Four storefronts are still lit. The first one is an insurance office with a man I reckon to be the owner at a desk toward the back. He wears a white shirt and blue trousers, with a gold chain around his tie. He smokes a pipe. "Why ya out so late, boy?"

"Selling tickets. The barnstorming Mississippi Mud Dogs and Kansas City River Kings professional baseball team play your locals in a game tomorrow. How many tickets do you want?"

"That's a good line. Yer a real hustler out this late." He blows a smoke ring to the ceiling. "Heard about this King team. Supposed to be good." He watches the smoke ring, then says, "Played a little ball myself in high school. Had a damn good arm. Could run like a deer in those days. Loved to hit." He shakes his head. "Ain't played since, sorry to say, though I meant to. Momma got sick. Had brothers and sisters to feed. Quit school." He looks at his cigar. "Now a wife. Kids. No time to do what I want. Work seven days a week. Fourteen hours a day." More smoke for the ceiling. "Always wondered was I as good as I thought."

He reaches into his pocket. "Give me seven tickets, boy."

I count them out. He hands me a two-dollar bill.

I say, "That's a buck seventy-five, sir. I owe you two bits. I only have fifteen cents change."

"Keep it. Don't spend it all in one place." We both laugh.

I thank him and turn to leave. At the door I look back. Mr. Insurance Man is somewhere other than his office. A faint smile on his face, he grips an imaginary bat and crouches like he's a batter waiting for the pitcher to throw him a fastball. He takes a mighty swing, then watches an imaginary ball soar high and far. Home run!

Next door the grocery store is about to close. They don't buy one ticket, but they do have peppermint sticks in the glass candy case. Two cents each. I buy five, put one in my ball glove for later, and pocket the brown sack the clerk hands me.

I hurry back to the camp and stop at Linda's tent. I say in a low voice, "It's Frankie. I have something for you."

"Don't you ever sleep?" She unzips the tent maybe two inches. I push the ticket money in, followed by the sack. She takes them both. "Now, good night, Frankie."

She must peek in the sack because I hear her giggle. She says, "Frankie Clothespin, you're a special person. This is a real treat. I hope the man I marry is as sweet as you."

I was hoping for a kiss but settled for a "thank you" filtered through the tent canvas.

27

Game Changers

Monday morning, Buell's purple Packard was parked outside Linda's tent, him wearing a gold Kings hat with a purple K outlined in gold. He wants me gone. I hunker down in the bushes outside her tent to hear them talk. Pops Buell's voice cracks like a pistol going off. "Dammit, woman, I said no. N.O. I don't need a big-bellied sheriff out to make a name for hisself throw me in jail for kidnappin' a white boy and takin' him 'cross state lines. They'd confiscate my vehicle. Take every dollar in my bank account. No thanks. The boy goes."

Buell reaches for the flap with a big hand. "I'm not the bad guy you think I am. I've been writin' letters and makin' telephone calls to Mexico, Canada—hell, Cuba even, tryin' to line up jobs for good ballplayers come next season. I got a center fielder who plays better defense than anyone in the Bigs but won't even get a tryout 'cause he's twenty-nine years old, has nine kids, and is colored. I got a third baseman, Bob Thorpe, who'd win a batting title in either league, but he stammers and stutters, so people think he's touched in the head. I got a pitcher who oughta be up. Great stuff, but she'll never face DiMaggio or Musial or Snider 'cause she's the wrong color. And sex." He smiles. "Mebbe the Clowns will sign ya. The white boy's gotta go."

"Can he stay till we're in Pittsburg, Kansas?" Linda asks. "He'll ride in Delray's car. My sister, Delphine, will be there. We'll drive him to his daddy's in Parsons after the game. Season's over then. Fair enough?"

Buell doesn't answer right away. Linda adds, "He's saved you money on groceries. He picked the blackberries for my cobbler.

Peaches for my pies. His ticket sales put twenty to thirty dollars in your pocket. He'll be gone in two days."

Buell speaks in a clear voice. "Yer cobblers and pies were fine. Ticket sales good. But he has to go. Hear? It's the end of the road for yer white boy," Buell says. "I ain't crossin' no state line with him in tow."

Linda smiles. "You sure? He found three good batting practice balls this week. That's six bucks in your pocket. And we didn't lose nary a ball either. What's that worth?"

The Kings use any field they can find during the week to practice on, usually a ballpark in colored town with chicken-wire backstops and gunnysack bases. Weeds and sassafras grow along the outfield fence. When a ball lands in high weeds, most of the Kings high-step away. I figure if I don't bother a snake, it won't bother me. Besides, most are harmless black snakes, not poisonous copperheads, or rattlers. I wade in, find the lost ball, and throw it to the batting practice pitcher.

"I can't just drive off and leave him," she says.

"Ain't that how ya found him?"

"Almost. But he's no trouble. Sleeps in trees. Helps without being asked. You liked my gooseberry pie, right? He picked the berries."

"You told me that, girl. I'm cuttin' him."

Linda says, "Since Frankie's white, he can go into businesses you and I can't. He's probably sold thirty tickets in offices. That's found money for you."

"But that didn't keep the KKK from visitin' us, now did it? He's traveled his last mile with my ball club."

Linda acts like she doesn't hear him. "He helps me a lot. Peels potatoes. Totes water. Takes coffee to Suitcase and Sam ever morning. Burns our trash, sweeps tent floors. Does what I ask without one whimper."

Buell gives her the stop sign like he's coaching third base. "Hush. I done said I ain't takin' no white kid 'cross the state line agin. Not after the Klan visit."

"We don't know that idiot was Klan."

"Now whose bein' stupid? Sure he was."

"Frankie was with us when we crossed into Missouri from Illinois."

"My mistake. I mistook him for one of Delray's kids. Never agin. His contract has run out."

"Since Jackie went to the Bigs, a dollar saved is a dollar earned."

Buell throws his hands in the air. "Thank you, Miss Linda Lou, for remindin' me we're in the sunset of a grand tradition. I've seen the coffins. We play two games a week nowadays and sell what, hundred fifty, two-hundred tickets? Used to be we'd play seven, eight games agin good teams, colored or white. Hell, Babe Ruth, Dizzy Dean, Bob Feller. They all barnstormed. I played agin them more 'n once. Held my own if I do say so. Those days we'd sell fifteen hundred, two thousand seats a game. Plus, shirts and caps by the carload. Other souvenirs. Today, we play piss-poor teams with piss-poor pitchers and fat-assed catchers and barely make gas money. We carry twelve players, not twenty-five. I have to rely on a girl's pitchin' exhibitions to make my nut."

He goes to the tent flap. "All this has no bearin' on the boy. He's out." He unzips the flap. "I'll go pick up Ruby, then we'll head out. That white boy better be gone when I'm back, hear."

Linda drives me to the Greyhound Station in Delray's car. "Sorry about Pop's decision. I figured he'd do this, so I bought you a ticket to Parsons yesterday." She hands me an envelope and two dollars.

I push the money away.

"Take it," she says. "Buy a Nehi. Sack of potato chips. Celebrate. It's a short ride to Parsons from here. Your daddy'll be glad to see you." Her eyelashes are wet.

My face feels frozen, yet the air's so hot I can hardly breathe.

"You're my kind of kid, Frankie Clothespin." She slips a card into my shirt pocket. "My address and telephone number. If things don't work out with your family, call me. Collect."

She smiles. "Delphine knows about you, Frankie. Says she'd like someone to mow our yard, rake leaves, cut wood, shovel snow, start a fire in the kitchen stove cold mornings." She laughs. "You'd go to school. Sleep in any tree you want. There's plenty on our street. We'll play lots of catch since I'm retiring from the Kings."

My throat aches. I'd like to hug her but squeeze her hand instead. She wipes her eyes. "Go. Or you'll miss your bus."

At the station door, I watch her drive off with a wave. I'm all alone. Again.

PART IV

Baseball is something more than a game to an American boy; it's his training field for life's work. Destroy his faith in its squareness and honesty and you have destroyed something more, you have placed suspicion of all things in his heart.

> —Kenesaw Mountain Landis, baseball's first commissioner who cleaned up the Black Sox scandal.

28

SQUEEZE PLAY

Inside the bus depot, a ceiling fan stirs hot air. Bright green flies flit in a shaft of sunlight. In the men's room I put Linda's note in my shoe, along with a dollar, then take a seat near the counter.

A tall guy wearing a white hat with a shiny black bill, horn-rimmed glasses, a white shirt with red lettering that reads Manager, gives me the once over. He played first base for the locals yesterday when big bad Jake Hazlett, who Linda made a fool of at her pitching demonstration, didn't show.

"How ya been?"

He hustles around the counter. "Yer in the White Folks section, boy. Move."

I laugh. "I'm White."

"Yer skin, yeah. But not blood. I seen ya with them coloreds yestriddy. Ya were birthed by that wench pitcher of theirs."

"Linda? She's not my momma, she's...my...friend. My momma died a long time ago. I'm white as you."

"Don't sass me, boy. Park yer Black ass in the colored section, or I'm callin' the law."

I'd like to punch his nose. Instead, I shrug and move behind a low wall beneath a sign that reads Colored Only. I've seen this sign a lot. That and Whites Folks Only. They're usually on restaurant windows, restroom doors, department store entrances, drinking fountains, movie theaters, even churches. Since I'm white, I'd never paid 'em any mind. Daddy neither, I guess. Now, I hate every word.

The chair I'm in has a cracked bottom, the nail head digging at my rear. It's too dark to see the clock on the wall, so I don't know how long till the bus comes. The store manager and I are the only ones in the station.

The town first baseman picks up the telephone and barks a number to the operator. He watches my every move, but turns his back when he speaks, so I know his conversation is about me. *Should I wait outside?*

A red-faced man in a green suit and a red necktie, dragging two suitcases, comes in, buys a ticket, and takes a seat in the white section. He and Mr. First Baseman agree the weather's hot, and fish won't bite since it's been a week since the last rain. The red-faced man scowls at me.

I smile. "Howdy."

"Shut yer yap, boy, or I'll close it fer ya."

The manager joins his laughter, picks up the telephone again and gives the operator a number, turning his back to me. Again. He's hot to tell someone he's seen me. Sweat pops out on my arms; my shirt sticks to my back.

I stand and head for the soda cooler.

Two guys, both big as King Kong, come through the bus station's revolving doors. They look at the manager. He jerks his head toward me. I open the cooler lid to pull out an RC. A big hand slams the lid shut. "That soda pop is for white folks, boy."

He twists my right arm behind my back. The other goon does the same with my left arm. "Yer ride's here." They both laugh.

They lift me outside, my legs dangling like a rag doll, and toss me into a pickup truck, tie my hands behind my back, and jam a paper sack over my head. The pickup speeds off, two ugly goons squeezing breath from my lungs.

29

Work the Count

"Ayak?" the goon who nabbed me says.

"Akia," another voice says.

"Kigy," says goon.

"And I thee," the man answers.

I hear backslaps. Daddy told me Klan members sometimes talk gibberish. This must be one of those times.

"Where's our Black boy?"

A boot slams into my ribs. "Right here. His mammy's that wench who pitched agin us yesterday. Claims he's white."

"Don't they all? Ain't nothin' worse than a darkie claimin' white."

Goon says, "You my relief? I got baby chicks and a load of wood to deliver. My ole lady expects a twenty-dollar bill this week."

His visitor snorts. "I hear ya. I got two bitches bitin' my butt too. Like money grows on trees. The Black one I'm tappin', and the woman who's the momma of my kids."

"Yer lucky ya got two kinds of stink. I ain't got but one. If'n I don't make them deliveries and bring her money, I won't have none. She wiggles for cash only."

"Hold yer horses, Knight. Ya know Klan bidness always comes first. Drink th' RC I brung ya and simmer down. I'll call a Nighthawk when I find a phone. They'll call the Grand Magi. He'll get in touch with the Grand Cyclops. They'll schedule a Firestone necklace for our Black friend."

"That's good. But I got deliveries to make. Need the bucks. Hear?"

"Said I'd take care of ya, didn't I? Okay?"

"When ya come back, bring rope. Cannin' jar rubbers work fine as handcuffs in a 'mergency, but rope's better."

The canning jar rubbers are thick, with not much give. They cut into my skin, turning my arms numb. If I get a thumb under one, maybe I can work it off and run, but that's hard to do lying on my back in the dirt.

"Ya search him?"

"Nah. He ain't packin'."

"Not fer guns, dummy. Fer money. Blackies don't go nowhere without a buck or two."

Rough hands roll me to my belly. They turn my pants pockets inside out. "See. What'd I tell ya? Dollar thirty. 'Nuff fer a plug of Star and a Griesedieck fer me and you." He giggles. "I'll see if I can get a refund on this bus ticket."

The two of them walk off, happy to split my money, I guess.

The visitor says, "I gotta shove Knight, now that you's fed and all. Orion."

"See if ya can get me relief. Hear? Orion, Knight."

More backslaps. They didn't find the dollar in my shoe or the paper with Linda's name and address. I remember the orphanage and the scars Sweeper had on his ass. His beatings are minor league compared to what these idiots have planned for me—a car tire around my neck, filled with gasoline and set on fire.

A robin's whistle brings me awake. The dust under me is wet with my sweat. A hot breeze stirs tree leaves. Cicadas drone. I can't feel my arms. My ass will soon sprout roots I've lain in one spot so long. I have to get out of this mess, but I don't know if the goon is still around.

"Hey. Third Base," I yell. "You hear me?"

"Shut the fuck up. I don't talk to darkies." He sounds close.

Daddy told me people like to talk about themselves. I'll try that. "You've got a good arm. Ever pitch?"

"Nah. Coach's son does that."

"With a better follow-through, you'd be good."

"Whatcha ya know 'bout pitchin'?"

I think of what Sis always said. *I change sides to lie.* I decide to go along with their story that I'm Little Linda's son. "My momma taught me. She can throw seven different pitches for strikes."

"I knew it! I knew ya was colored. We're gonna burn yer ass, Black boy."

"You still oughta pitch." I'll go down fighting.

"Shut yer mouth. Blackies and me don't talk, 'member?"

His boot slams into my ribs.

30

Intentional Walk

Roots dig into my back. My arms ache. Ants crawl on my belly. I itch all over. I scoot so as to get my shoulders against the tree trunk, my fingers still digging at the canning rubbers around my wrists.

When I'm free, I'll run and run and run. Where I'll run, I don't know. Just run.

Sweat burns my eyes. The air in the paper bag is hot to my lungs. Crows caw. A cow moos. A train whistle sounds. I'm helpless as a rabbit in a trap.

I wish I were playing center field for the Cardinals with Stan "The Man" Musial in right field and Enos "Country" Slaughter in left. We'd catch every fly ball hit out of the infield. Harry Caray, the Cards radio announcer, will be at the microphone: "The Redbird's classy left-hander, Harry 'The Cat' Breechen, winds and pitches. The batter swings. It's a humpback liner to short center. Walker races in, dives, and gloves the ball. Holy cow, what a catch!"

The goon yells, "Who ya talkin to, boy? Ya nuts? Ya said I need a better follow-through. What's wrong with mine?"

"Bend your back more. You'll get better leverage."

"Like this?"

"Can't see through this sack."

"What the hell. Ya seen me, anyway." He pulls the sack off my head.

Sunlight stabs my eyes. The fresh air cools my face. I squint and make out four forked poles set in the ground, with tree limbs woven together and branches piled on top of them to form a brush arbor like at that three-day foxhunt Daddy took me to last year. Wood benches face a fire ring. Three chairs, with the middle one the tallest, face one of the stands like preachers use in church. The goon says, "Watch this."

He takes a rock from a big pile he gathered in the grass. He faces an oak tree, circles his right arm three times, rears back, brings his left arm across his body, and lunges forward, staggering like a drunk, fat jiggling. The rock misses his target a good three feet.

"Ya see that? Just like Vic Raschi."

I've never seen Vic Raschi pitch, but I'm sure no New York Yankee hurler is as clumsy as Goon. "Rock more on your left foot when you lift your arms."

"Like this?" He throws again. The stone sails wide.

"That's better. Form leads to function." As Little Linda says. "Practice your delivery. Don't worry about results. When your form's right you'll throw strikes." More of Linda's advice.

"Ya think so?"

"Sure. Practice. Concentrate on your form."

He grins, winds and throws, grunting and stumbling each time. Twice, his rock nicks the oak. Once, it hits solid.

"Hey! I'm gettin' good!"

"What's goin' on here?" asks a man's voice.

The goon, his face red and sweaty, answers, "Practicin' pitchin', pastor."

They know each other since they don't talk gibberish. "A Devil's game, baseball." He points at me. "Cover that boy's eyes."

The pastor carries a rubber tire, a gas can, and a lunch box.

My world turns black when the goon pulls the sack over my head.

"You my relief?" he asks the pastor.

"No, Knight. I gotta a funeral to preach. Then handle a dispute between the ladies in the quiltin' society. Ya know the trouble women cause us men."

He hits something with his fist. "Our boy's necklace. Wednesday night's the ceremony." That's two days away.

"How old ya figure Blackie is?" the pastor says.

"Eight, maybe nine. Smart little shit. Too bad he's gonna die."

I'm eleven, you goon. Too young to die.

"Most Blacks ain't got the sense God gave a sinner. Why's this boy different?'

"Talks like a white man," the goon says. "Ya bring rope?"

"Didn't know it were needed. Barney said we caught us a Black boy. Grabbed an old tire and gasoline. Brung ya fried chicken. Coffee."

The goon says, "Much obliged."

The preacher laughs and says, "Put this tire 'round his arms. Ya won't need rope then. Come sundown Wednesday we'll fill it with gas, light a match, and watch him crawl and beg."

The smell of sun-heated rubber makes me gag. The tire pins my arms to my body. The goon says, "Dammit, preacher, I need relief. I've got deliveries waitin' to be made. My old lady expects a twenty-dollar bill come Friday. I don't get it, I'm up shit creek."

"Ssshhush. No black guardin', Knight." He pauses. "I unnerstand yer problem. Here's mine. With so many Citizens off followin' the harvest money trail, I'm shorthanded. Even had to call Illinois for a Kludd."

"Ain't ya th' chaplain?"

"I'm Grand Magi. 'Member?"

"Sorry, fergot."

A plop in the dust and the smell of tobacco juice. The goon's favorite trick. This one missed me by inches.

"I got work to do. Deliveries to make. Mouths to feed."

"Relax, Knight. My boy'll be here soon's school's out. Then ya can go. Till then, eat yer chicken. Drink yer coffee. Stop frettin'."

"I'm serious. My missus gotta have twenty bucks this week."

"No one said the gate to Heaven opens without sacrifice. 'Member, yer doin' God's work, Knight."

When next he speaks his words sound farther away. "Orion, Knight."

The goon says, "Orion. I reckon."

The heavy tire turns my arms to lead. I wiggle so that more weight rests on my shoulders, trying to keep my arms from going numb. As I move I feel a jar rubber move too. I could yell with happiness. I slip my thumb under the rubber and twist. My right hand comes free.

Behind me, the goon cusses. "Fried chicken, my ass. Back. Wings. Cold coffee. Ya'd think in the year ninety hundred and fifty they could make a thermos that would at least keep coffee warm."

I hear liquid hit the ground, followed by the bang of a garbage-can lid. Then, Goon's footsteps on the gravel path going away. Seconds later, a door hinge creaks, followed by a door closing. The goon's in the privy. Now's my chance.

I lift the tire, pull my left hand free, tear off the sack, jump to my feet, and run like I'm Sudden Sam stealing second base. It's been so long since I walked, my feet burn. My heels hurt. The sun blinds my eyes. I race past the oak tree and bust through poison ivy and sumac and into a stand of trees. My feet slip on ash and oak leaves, but I keep my legs churning. Briars slash my hands. A may apple vine hooks my foot and slams me to the ground, knocking wind from my lungs. I lie still till I can breathe, then crawl over toadstools through horseweeds and cow cabbage, flint shards knifing into my hands, cutting my jeans.

At the top of the hill, two sycamores grow beside a gully. I follow the ditch downhill to a slough of black water filled with dying cottonwoods and sycamores. The train track must be beyond the berm.

Dragonflies dart and flit on the green scum covering the slough. A snapping turtle shows his pointed head.

The water is too deep to wade. I'd dog paddle but the water moccasins would have me in three strokes. I'm duck soup if I stay where I am. I have a choice—Firestone necklace or find Daddy in Kansas.

When I worked for Simms Tree Trimming, before Sis locked

me away in the orphanage, at lunchtime we'd ride saplings for fun. If you climb a young ash or hickory it'll sway under your weight, but not break. You lean right, it goes that way. Throw your weight left, it swoops that direction. Keep at it and they'll bend faster and faster, almost touching the ground, then spring back the other way. It's a rough, fun ride. A country boy's roller coaster, we called it.

A slender hickory grows at water's edge. I shimmy up it and lean forward. It dips. I pull back. It bends with my weight. I repeat my movements. Each time the sapling swoops faster and lower. When it looks like murky water will swallow me, I let go and jump, kicking my feet, flailing my arms to carry me farther in the air. I land with a thud in a thicket of buck brush on the other side.

Everything goes black. When I come to with ants crawling in the leaves by my nose, I sit up. My shirt's torn, my jeans ripped. The scratches on my arms ooze blood. I bruised my right leg, but other than that, I seem fine. I crossed the slough, but there are no weeds or trees to hide me. Goon and his gang will spy me in a hurry unless I move. I climb the berm, pulling myself up on weeds and tree roots.

From the top, I see silver railroad tracks running east. My escape route? I'll do my walk a hundred, run a hundred steps trick like the night I bolted from the orphanage. The train trestle up ahead would make a good hiding place, but I know they'll watch that like a farmer watches storm clouds. Search parties will scour this area, looking under every rock, jumping on each fallen tree. They'll cover every part of that trestle.

I limp through knee-high grass to a drainage ditch that leads to a stand of cottonwoods. The trestle's to my left maybe fifty yards away. I'll climb a cottonwood, wait for dark, then follow the rails to a highway, thumb a ride from a traveling salesman or trucker, go to Kansas, and find Daddy.

But first, eats. The creek is spring fed with a clay bottom. I follow it uphill to a draw where wild strawberries grow. The berries are small and bitter, but I stuff them in my mouth as fast as I can chew. On the eastern slope I dig wild potatoes and wild onions. I pull them from the soft dirt, wipe them clean on my pants, and chew them with pepper grass.

When I'm full and pretty sure I haven't been followed, I stretch out in the grass. I wonder what Sis would say if she saw me now. She would have a conniption. I'm filthy, my jeans and shirt caked with mud. There's a nice pool of water under a willow tree. I pull my jeans and shirt off and wash them in the cold water, then spread them dripping wet on the grass for the sun to dry. The breeze feels good on my back and bare butt. My right knee throbs from tiny cuts, but otherwise I'm fine. I stretch out in the warm clover. The smell of violets and lilacs reminds me of Little Linda after she's showered. Clouds float in a blue sky. The sun and the gentle breeze make shadows dance on the grass. Bees buzz in the clover. It's a great day for baseball. Perfect temperature. No wind to help curveballs break more. The Kings play in Pittsburg, Kansas, today and tomorrow, with Linda on the mound.

Someday, she and I will play for the Cards, with me at short-stop. I see it now. A three-game series at Sportsman Park in St. Louis in late September, against the Brooklyn Dodgers. Who-ever wins two out of three goes to the World Series to play the New York Yankees. Jackie Robinson comes to bat. Linda winds and fires. Jackie swings. It's a hard ground ball to my left. I dive, glove the ball, scramble to my feet, and fire to first.

Yer out, the ump yells.

Linda slaps my hand. Great play, Frankie.

I grin and reach for a clover stem to suck on, like Delray does when he goes to the outfield for the Kings.

A boot comes from nowhere and smashes my hand. Hard. The sun blinds me, but I recognize that boot. It's Skinny, the KKK guy who tried to force his way on Linda.

31

OUT AT HOME

It was a cold, windy day when Daddy came home from Yellowbird. He'd been gone four days, leaving me with two cans of Spam, a scrapping of flour, three hounds, and three cups of dog food. No sugar. No Karo. No Carnation.

I dug cow cabbage and dandelion roots from the frozen ground down by the creek and boiled the tough, stringy things. They tasted muddy and hot to the tongue, but it was better than nothing.

The yard gate creaked. I heard cuss words, then Daddy busted through the back door, like he was being chased. He looked the worse for wear. His coat sleeve hung by a thread. His shirt was ripped. His overalls torn. His face was covered with red and purple bruises. Blood was caked under his nose, his lips black. He smelled of sweat and piss, and needed a shave.

"I'm home, Frankie," he said, as if he was a birthday present for me or something. "Had a rough go." The black gap in his gum had held a tooth the last time I saw him. "Sold Jim. Left groceries at Rabbit's Gap. Ya feed the dogs?"

"Yesterday. Ain't nothin' left to feed 'em."

"Brung some."

We needed two mules to pull our wagon and drag logs. "How much did you get for him?"

"Ya hunt while I were gone?" he said.

"No, sir."

"Good. Fresh dogs run better. Go fetch them groceries, then stir us up a bite. We'll go chase a fox."

"In daylight?"

"Don't hector, boy. Do."

It was the first time he'd been cross with me in ages.

Daddy wiped his face with scarred knuckles. "Twenty-seven bucks. Jim's worth more. But needed cash. Still got four singles." Daddy got snookered on that deal for sure.

I pulled on my coat and ran to Rabbit's Gap. The grocery sack hung from a fence post. Back in the kitchen I found a can of ground pepper, a jar of peanut butter, two cans of Spam, a can of Pet Milk, a box of shredded coconut, a chunk of baloney, a jar of mustard, two sticks of oleo, a box of lime Jell-O, and a small bag of dog food.

No Karo syrup. No bacon. And I wondered how we'd eat Jell-O, but I zipped my lip and fried baloney in oleo, smeared it with peanut butter, and set the plate before Daddy, hoping maybe he'd use his four bucks for corn meal, lard, and Karo tomorrow or the next day.

Daddy gulped down my cooking, licked peanut butter off his fingers, and said, "Let's hit the woods. I wanna hear my dogs run."

An orange ball of a sun hung in the sky when we turned the dogs loose on the ridge. They headed for the creek that cut through our pasture. In maybe ten minutes, Dinah's liberty-bell squall let us know she was onto a fox. Stub and Little Bit joined her. They crossed the creek, circled juniper trees, and headed west, giving mouth every time their feet hit the ground.

Daddy said, "When I die, if heaven don't got music this sweet, I wanna go the other way."

We splashed through cold creek water, ducking oak limbs to a hilltop overlooking the creek bottom. The dogs had lost the scent of Ol' Red. We watched Dinah and Little Bit puzzle through a blackberry patch, trying to figure out which way the fox had run.

Stub mouthed on the ridge. Dinah and Little Bit joined him in minutes. The three hounds raced downhill, passing maybe twenty-five yards away in full cry.

"Whoopee," Daddy yelled. "Don't this beat all?"

When the dogs swung north, out of hearing distance, we didn't run to catch up. Before I could ask why, Daddy said,

"Need a break." That was a first for him. He squatted like a baseball catcher next to a walnut tree. He could sit that way for hours. Hunkerin', he called it.

"The mule's a noble beast," he said. That's all, like he grabbed those words from the air. He cocked his head, trying to hear the hounds, but it was only the wind in the trees and the rustle of weeds.

A long five minutes passed. "Had a beer at the Blue Moon," Daddy said. "This blow-hard town guy comes in blackguardin' ever which way, askin' fer trouble. Me and Trace Galloway was the onliest ones there. Guy calls us stupid rednecks. You know Trace. He's pretty much a runt in size and no fighter. Slips out the side door. This feller says, 'See, you all is cowards and chicken shits.'

"Loudmouth brags he can whup five rednecks at the same time and not work up a sweat. He blackguards me to a fair-thee-well. Pisses me off. I invite him outside. We square off 'neath that tall maple tree by the Blue Moon. Folks come over from Pat's Grocery and the post office. This fella has forty pounds and five inches on me. Hits like a fallin' tree. He whups me real bad till I lay one under his chin. His feet get tangled. He falls. Smacks his head agin a root or somethin', I reckon. Don't move, 'cept his right leg. It quivered and jerked. Oncet."

Daddy looked to the sky like he expected a lightning bolt. "Feller just lays there, mouth half open. Somebody calls, *Throw water on him.* Ain't got none. So, I piss on him. He don't move. Harley Stevenson comes up, has hisself a look and says, 'Ya kilt him, Mick.' Harley runs to the post office to call the law. Half hour, forty-five minutes later, Deputy Branch swaggers up and tosses me in the slammer. Second degree murder."

Daddy shook his head to clear away the memory. "Spent the night in the hoosegow. Yestriddy afternoon the sheriff comes in. Says he talked to them who watched the whole shebang. Said I acted in self-defense. Still, sheriff made me stay in his Gray-Bar Hotel till the judge heard my case this mornin'. Sheriff tells the judge he's droppin' charges."

It flabbergasted me to hear Daddy string together so many words. His usual total was ten or fifteen. A month. It's not news that he fought when he drank. That he killed a man gobsnockered me to a fair-thee-well. But Daddy didn't seem bothered.

Daddy said, "After some legal mumblin's this mornin', Judge Williamson said he'd take the sheriff's recommendation this once and let me go. Said if I even look cross-eyed at 'nother human an' he hears 'bout it, he'll put my ass in jail and throw away the key. Said I owe the county ten bucks fer disturbin' the peace and five dollars court costs. Said I were to leave town and stay gone."

Daddy looked at his wrists like they were new. "'Fore the sheriff took his cuffs off, he given me thirty days to pay my fines. If'n I don't, he says I'll spend spring and summer, maybe fall, in his caboose."

Daddy shook his head again, like the nightmare'd returned. "Says I'm to never ever step one foot in the Blue Moon." He looked to the sky again. "Jail's a bad place, boy. Hard bed. Cold floor. Awful food."

Daddy stood and kicked at a clump of broom grass. "Never meant that fella no harm. But I couldn't sit there and let him call me a lily-white coward, could I?"

He pulled his coat closer. "Went to get Jim. Weren't where I'd tied him. Folks said the schoolmarm took him. Went to her house."

The schoolteacher he speaks of is Doris Ann Foy. Miss Doris. She buys mushrooms from us in the spring and blackberries in the summer.

Daddy tried to laugh. "That blame woman said, 'The mule is a noble beast.' Said I were a worthless son-of-a-gun leavin' a fine animal with no food or water. Tole her I were in jail. 'More reason you shouldn't own a mule. Or raise a boy. You can't take care of yourself, much less another living soul.'"

Killing and going to jail aren't Christian acts. Daddy knew this 'cause his face was pale as ash bark, his eyes aglitter. "That danged womin opened her pocketbook an' counted out twenty-seven smackeroos. Cash money. 'I'm buying that mule right this very minute.'"

Daddy stood and leaned against the tree. "Got a terrible headache, boy. Won't go away. Brassy taste in my mouth." He coughed and spit.

"Jim's as good a mule as ya'll ever see. Worth fifty bucks at least. Still, needed her money bad, so we shook. Paid the sheriff his ten and five dollars for the judge. Went to the store. Bought grub. Come home."

I knew this was the last time Daddy would ever say a word about this fight. He's not big on talking about certain things, like Momma and her health, though I've asked him more than once. He'll talk about mules a lot.

Once we were giving them a blow after pulling a wagonload of corn uphill.

"A mule comes 'bout when a female horse, a mare, gets bred by a male donkey, a jack," he said, and then he went quiet, figuring, I reckon, that such talk wasn't fit for my young ears.

Another time he said, "Mules live longer'n horses. Hell, Jim and Jude were a team five, maybe six years 'fore I bought 'em. That were fifteen years or so ago."

That day he'd seemed in a talking mood, so I asked about Momma.

"Sickly most of the time. Died when you were what, four?"

We'd been skidding logs down the creek and a log rammed a buried rock. Jim and Jude had stopped pulling that very instant.

"Have to dig us free or we'll stand here all day," Daddy said. When the log was free, he said, "Folks think mules are stubborn. Not true. They just won't do stupid stuff, is all. Like try to pull what can't be pulled. Or cross a bridge that ain't safe. If a rattlesnake's in yer path, a mule will wait for it to crawl away. A horse will go white-eyed and crazy at the smell of a copperhead. Not a mule. They'll eat most anything and still work hard."

So that day when he said, "Never meant the fella no harm," I knew that was all his way of saying the fight was over and so was his talk. I figured that since he was finished talking about his fight, we'd chase after the hounds like usual. Instead, we stood under a gray sky and watched brown leaves skitter before a cold wind carrying the smell of snow.

Daddy took a deep breath. "I tell ya, boy. Foxhuntin's sure better 'n jail."

Then it got quiet as a cemetery at midnight. After a while, Dinah rang her liberty-bell mouth in the hollow below us. We won't have to run after our dogs, I reckoned.

"Ain't she a good 'un?" Daddy said, slapping his leg with his cap. He took four short steps, then flopped face first in the weeds like a bale of hay falling from a hayloft.

"Why'd ya do that?" I yelled.

It was like he didn't hear me.

I rolled him over. His blue eyes were gray. Spittle covered his lips. He breathed fast, and he was wet with sweat. I knew he needed a doctor, but I had no idea how to get him to one.

Volney had a hospital, but it was eighteen or twenty miles away. A long pull, even for Jude. Yellowbird was only three, four miles the way a crow flies, but over crooked, muddy roads it's twice that far. Still, it was my best choice. Even if the sheriff said Daddy was to stay out of Yellowbird, I didn't think he'd keep a sick man from catching a ride to a hospital. Daddy had four bucks, which I hoped would buy enough gas to get us to Volney once we got to Yellowbird.

I ran home, went to the kennel, poured dog food in three bowls, and added baloney, so the hounds would have something to eat when they came home. Inside, I yanked the oilcloth off the kitchen table and pulled curtains from the front room windows to wrap Daddy in.

I dropped a can of Spam in my coat pocket and dumped Carnation milk into an empty Karo pail, added Jell-O and shredded coconut. Jude's supper. She's not a riding mule, so I knew I'd have to use the red wagon we used to carry chips and kindling from the wood lot to the house.

Jude was in the barn, her head hanging low like she missed Jim. I pulled the harness from its peg and climbed on the feed trough so I was tall enough to slip the collar over Jude's ears and down her neck. I put on her harness, snapped the tail strap, buckled the back straps, and pulled the belly band tight. She took the bit easy as usual, and I snapped the reins to it.

"We have to get Daddy to the hospital," I said to Jude. "We'll go through Yellowbird. I need your help, understand?"

Jude craned her head when I roped the cellar door to the wagon and tied the wagon handle to the trace chain. Daddy was where I'd left him, his face gray, eyes closed. Using two walnut limbs, I rolled him like a log, tucking the tablecloth with each roll. Using a rock as a fulcrum, I lifted him onto the door in the wagon.

Jude watched with big brown eyes. When the tablecloth caught on a wagon rail, keeping Daddy from settling on the door, she pulled the wagon forward. Daddy's body fit the door neat as a skillet in an oven. He was right. Mules were smart.

I tucked the curtains under Daddy's chin, tied them off, and circled the rope around the wagon.

"Next stop, Yellowbird," I said. Jude seemed to understand.

Who'd help us once we were in Yellowbird? Who had a car? Would snow make the roads too slick to travel? I pushed these questions away and followed Jude along the ridgeline and across an open field to a rutted logging road. Going downhill, I hung on so the wagon wouldn't run into Jude's back feet. Uphill, I pushed.

The road forked. Jude turned north. Jude tossed her head when I pulled the reins south.

"C'mon, girl. Let's go south." Then I remembered what Daddy'd said. *Once a mule's been someplace, they never forget how to get there.* "Okay, gal. You're the boss. Let's go to Yellowbird."

Jude's hooves sliced through weeds, mud, and sleet. The air smelled of moldy leaves and wet weeds. At a brush pile Jude turned north again, path no wider than a game trail.

We bumped over rocks and tree limbs to a long downgrade. I tripped, losing my grip on the wagon, and it picked up speed. The trace chain went slack. Jude trotted, then loped, shying to one side. The wagon went faster, plowing through weeds and shrubs. Ropes flew in the air. The cellar door went sailing, slamming into broom grass and buck brush.

I jumped up and ran to Daddy, who was on his back. He'd landed on part of the cellar door. He moaned but seemed unhurt.

I wiped sleet from his face and pulled him onto the door. The wagon had a dent on one side, but the axle worked fine, and the wheels turned when I said, "Get up, girl." From there I saw that if Jude hadn't shied like she did, Daddy and the wagon would have been at the bottom of a deep, rock-filled gully. Daddy might have been hurt bad, even killed.

I rubbed Jude's nose. "Good girl. You're a noble beast."

I used the fulcrum-and-limb trick to get Daddy and the door back in the wagon. This time I tied the ropes with double, half-hitch knots. The wind had moved to the north. Weeds and grass were covered with ice and snapped off when stepped on. Chickadees and snowbirds fought to get the seeds. Sleet pellets stung my face. I worried about Jude, but Daddy'd told me a mule's skin was not as sensitive as that of a horse. Still, if she got hurt, all was lost.

Jude pulled up a draw to a stand of trees at the top. The wind was strong there. Ice crystals, blown from the trees, made holes in the snow. Each step was slippery, yet Jude took us across a small stream. She stopped on the other side, snow and sleet swirling. Something was wrong. I didn't cluck at her or shake the reins. I'd learned my lesson. I'd just wait.

Then, like a screech owl's call mixed with a bolt of lightning, a walnut limb twisted from a tall tree and crashed across our path, sending leaves and branches into the air. If we hadn't stopped, those heavy limbs would have killed us. Jude's smarts had saved us again.

She watched patiently as I removed what limbs I could off

our path, then with dainty steps she tugged the wagon around
the crashed limbs and branches and over to a stand of cedars,
where she stopped. Using Daddy's barlow I cut branches, shook
off the sleet, and covered Daddy with them. Jude stood still as
I layered the sweet-smelling cedar across her back, shoulders,
and neck, and tied them down. She stamped her feet when I
finished, like she was saying thanks.

While we were stopped, I held the Karo pail to Jude's muzzle. She made quick work of the Carnation milk, Jell-O, and
coconut flakes. I opened my can of Spam and chewed it cold,
wishing I had some water.

Daddy looked monster-big on my little red wagon covered
with cedar limbs, and when Dinah gave mouth in the hollow
below us, he moaned and waved his arms.

"Ain't she something," Daddy'd said earlier.

Now, I nodded in agreement. What a dog Dinah is. She'd
stayed after her fox in this storm. Alone. Stub and Little Bit
were safe and warm in the kennel, I imagined. I figured Dinah
would stick with Ol' Red till he holed up.

I'd been in these woods before. The road skirted Coal Bin
Holler for maybe a mile, crossed Middle River Bridge, and hit
the blacktop just north of Huffmaster's Hill. From there it was
a mile or so to Yellowbird.

Dinah's liberty-bell mouth rang clear from there. She'd been
my special buddy since that spring day six or seven years before,
when Daddy had brought her and Stub home. They were full
brother and sister. Daddy got them from a foxhunter in Ten-
nessee. He was so excited about his purchase that even Momma had watched from the porch in her pink bathrobe. Daddy
turned the two black, lemon, and white pups loose. All floppy
ears and big feet, they tumbled and scrambled as I chased them
from flower bed to swinging gate.

Every morning Dinah greeted me with a wet kiss, and we
raced each other through the yard. When I went to answer na-
ture's call, she waited outside the privy, and she nipped my heels
when we trotted to the garden to pick tomatoes. She chased

grasshoppers with me, followed me to the chicken house when I gathered eggs, and curled up beside me in the sun and slept, her head on my belly. Right before Momma went away, she'd said Dinah was as good a mother as a boy could ask for.

Foxhound puppies behave differently than other pups—you can't teach them to fetch or play hide-and-seek or roll over for treats. They're bred to hunt, and from that first day they'd head to the kennel, bite the older dogs' tails, ride their backs, and nip their flanks. When they were four months old and Daddy took the older dogs to the woods, he'd tie Dinah and Stub to the wood pile to keep them from running with the big hounds so they wouldn't strain their muscles and be crippled for life.

Daddy said the worst thing a foxhound could do was run rabbits. "Ruins 'em for fox chases. If 'n one of my hounds takes off after a rabbit, I'll kill that dog when I find him."

One sunny morning Dinah and I were walking to the garden. A rabbit jumped up, and Dinah made a beeline for him. The cottontail hopped through the fence. Dinah, going lickety-split, hit the woven wire hard, knocking her to the ground. She got up, and limped to me, whimpering and whining, expecting a "Good girl."

Instead, I took her muzzle in my hand and looked her in the eye. "No. No. Bad dog."

Her eyes went deep black, she lowered her head. The next day, Stub pranced along when Dinah and I went to the wood lot. A rabbit bolted from a weed patch, a gray blur on green grass. Stub streaked off after Mr. Cottontail. Inches from catching the rabbit, Dinah jumped on Stub's back, growling, sinking sharp teeth into his neck.

Stub got the message. That was the last rabbit he ever chased. Daddy bragged to others. "My dogs don't lie," he'd say. "If they open up, you know for a fact it's a fox."

Now, on the road above Coal Bin Hollow, Jude pulled the wagon as Dinah gave mouth, trailing her fox alongside Middle River Creek, through a cornfield, across a pasture, and uphill toward the paved road.

That bothered me, since shoe-factory workers drove through there mornings and evenings going to work in Volney and coming home. Folks who lived in Yellowbird and worked in Jeff City traveled this road twice a day, five days a week. Overloaded logging trucks groaned up these long hills, hoping to avoid the highway patrol. From time to time I saw headlights sweep the trees above us, folks eager to get home and out of the weather.

At a grove of hickory trees I pulled Jude to a stop and checked Daddy's ropes, wiped melted sleet from his face, and tucked in his covers. We'd gone maybe fifty yards when Dinah gave three long squalls, her signal that Mister Fox was holed up.

For the first time in a long time I relaxed a little. Dinah'd go home now unless she smelled me. If she got my scent, she'd come in, belly rubbing the ground; circle me three times like usual; and wait for me to pat her head and tell her what a good dog she was. Then she'd follow along to Yellowbird. If that happened, I'd find a hunter to care for her till Daddy was back in the woods.

We waited under a big oak, sleet pelting the bare limbs like buckshot. When Dinah didn't come after five minutes or so, I figured she'd headed home. I clucked to Jude. She pulled the wagon through wet leaves, black mud, and sleet-covered grass, the wind ripping at tree limbs so fierce even crows wouldn't fly. We were almost to the gravel road. Wood smoke from houses in Yellowbird mixed with the fog and hung like blue gauze.

There was a loud squeal, maybe a screech owl or a lightning strike, or maybe a car slammed on its brakes. I listened for voices and heard none.

Jude picked her way slowly. Water from the flooded road ditch gushed downhill, carrying tree limbs, logs, and small rocks. One careful step at a time, we made our way to the blacktop.

At the pavement, Jude stopped, her feet planted. I'd seen this before. She wouldn't move until whatever was wrong was fixed. A howl split the air. My eyes searched the blacktop. The road was clear, except for a white clump that lay in the wet grass. Steam rose and black blood oozed from it. Dinah.

32

THE COUNT

Miss Doris and her husband lived in the yellow house with spiraea and oleander bushes in the yard, two houses south of the grain elevator in Yellowbird. That spring when I'd knocked to sell her mushrooms, she bought my whole bucket for three bucks and threw in some old *Life Magazines* to boot.

She came to the door in house robe and slippers.

"Hello. I'm Franklin Delano Walker. You bought a mule from my daddy yesterday. I brung you his harness mate, today. Jude and Jim have been together for over fifteen years."

She shook her head, which was covered in a halo of white hair. "The past participle of bring, is brought. Not brung. 'I bring a gift today. I brought you a gift yesterday.' Brung is incorrect usage."

When I didn't answer, she put her hands on her hips and said, "I paid your daddy a fair price for his mule. I don't have money for another one."

"I'll swap you Jim's harness mate for a ride to the hospital for my Daddy. And a vet for my dog."

"Hospital? Why?"

She pulled on a sweater, grabbed her glasses, and followed me outside. Jude stood solid as a soldier over the wagon, Daddy tied to the cellar door, Dinah between his legs.

I pushed the cedar fronds off Daddy. "Flopped down this afternoon. Ain't talked or walked since."

She touched Daddy's gray face and made a clicking sound. "Probably a stroke."

Tears ran down her face when she saw Dinah. "Ralph," she called. "Can you come out here, please?"

Her husband, Ralph, was a coon hunter. He came out and

looked first at Daddy, then at Dinah. He lifted the dog's head and touched her hip where white bone showed.

"No hope for your dog, boy. Your daddy needs a doctor. Fast." He lifted Dinah to his chest. She whined, her eyes closed.

"She's quite a foxhound, I hear. Truck hit her?"

I knew I'd cry if I answered, so I just nodded. Seeing Daddy fall and not get up to walk or talk, then finding my Dinah hurt and in pain, sent knife stabs to my heart.

Ralph said, "I'll bury her next to my Gabe. He was a hell of a coonhound, ya know." A good coonhound will tree maybe forty coons a season. I'd heard Gabe treed a hundred or a hundred twenty some years.

About then Jim brayed hello to Jude. She answered and pulled the wagon to the fence. They stood muzzle to muzzle, talking mule talk. Two neighbor men came up and carried Daddy to the garage.

"Your father needs a doctor fast," Miss Doris said.

I went to the fence and rubbed Jude's nose. "Thanks, girl. Without you, we'd never have made it." Her eyes went soft, then she nudged me with her head, as if to say, *Go finish your business.* I climbed into the car and pulled Daddy's feet to my lap.

As we were driving away, a rifle sounded from behind the barn. Goodbye, Dinah.

33

THE SLIP PITCH

At the hollow below the KKK camp, Skinny grips my neck so hard I can't breathe. I'm dizzy, naked, and cold. I'm tired, but know I need to stay awake.

Skinny smells like a gut wagon. He has a black eye from Linda's fists. He'll think twice before he tries to have his way with her again. Skinny limps when he walks, probably because his back hurts where I whammed him good. He wraps his belt around my feet and shoves me to the ground in a patch of persimmon sprouts, pulls out his knife and cuts a sprout about eight inches from its fork, trimming leaves to make a yoke. He puts it around my neck. When he squeezes the two ends together, the pain drops me to my knees.

Linda was right. I should've done him in like she begged. Another pop or two from my bat would have saved the world from this idiot. Daddy killed a man in a fight, and the judge agreed it was self-defense. Would the sheriff here agree that killing a white KKK member to defend a Black lady's virtue was self-defense? I doubt it. Skinny's lucky my bat hit his back, not his head.

I figure he'll drag my ass to the KKK camp. They'll tie me to a tree and guard me night and day until its Firestone-necklace time. The yoke is tight around my neck. By twisting the two limbs together, the pain makes me go where Skinny wants me to go.

He leads me along the railroad track, sharp rocks cutting into my bare feet. He smiles big, his teeth crooked. "Yes siree, JP Ettler captured the prize. JP Ettler found what the Knights lost. Now JP will get his rewards."

The rails hum. A train whistle blows as it crosses the trestle not a hundred yards away. "I could tie ya to the rails and let the wheels grind ya up," Skinny says. He laughs. "That'd be no fun. You'd die too fast. Ya gotta suffer and cry for mercy."

He twists the limbs. Pain shoots down my neck and across my shoulders. "I could break yer neck if I wanted, boy." I can't answer. "We'll wait here till the train passes."

He slaps his chest. "Them Knights been searchin' haystacks and log piles fer ya all day. JP Ettler grabbed ya easy as pullin' a possum from a tree. Told 'em I'd find ya. Yessiree. JP Ettler keeps his word."

The train speeds toward us fast. Skinny says, "No darkie pulls a gun on JP Ettler and lives to tell about it. No siree."

I don't say it was Sudden Sam who waved the gun at him, not me. JP Ettler doesn't want the truth. His mind is on the glory he'll get from bringing me back to the KKK.

The ground rumbles. Weeds and scrubs move in the wind. The whistle blows again. Passenger trains travel fast, blowing chaff and chat from its wheels. If I stay as Skinny's prisoner, I'll be burned alive. What if I dive across the tracks as the train passes? If I'm chewed to pieces who cares? Why live? Daddy's in far-away Kansas. He'll never know. My favorite foxhound, Dinah, is dead. Sis admitted me to an orphan's home. Little Linda, the greatest baseball pitcher I've ever seen, is quitting the game. I'm naked and cold. Broke. Hungry.

The train's fifty feet, then forty, then twenty-five feet away. I drop to my knees fast, jerk hard on the yoke and twist. It splinters in Ettler's hands. I sprint for the tracks and dive. My body sails across the track seconds before the silver wheels scream past. Railroad chat rips my skin. I roll down the embankment through horseweeds and poison oak and cow cabbage to a drainage ditch. I've got maybe ninety seconds until Ettler chases after me. Fast as a mink, I crawl over sand, through cobwebs and tree roots, past a black snake eating a mouse, as grasshoppers and katydids explode into the air and blackberry vines grab at me. My hands and knees sting and burn, and my arms hurt.

Mudholes tell me I'm in a creek bed. I collapse into a pool of murky water, my lungs trying to escape my chest.

I'd love to see JP Ettler's face right this minute. I bet he's one surprised fool. His prized captive escaped. Gone. Vanished. Ain't that too bad, Mr. Ettler? I smile, which turns into a giggle. Then, way down deep in my throat, my laugh box overturns. I guffaw until snot runs from my nose and tears flood my eyes. It's the funniest thing in the world that I'm naked as a newborn bird, that my knees bleed and my face is scratched. I laugh that the soles of my feet are cut to shit, that I have no shoes. It's hilarious that I'm broke, that I don't know where I am or how I'll get to Kansas, or even what town Daddy lives in. It's a scream that I'm tired, hungry, and alone. I laugh that I'm alive, sitting in a mudhole in a ditch and the Ku Klux Klan thinks I'm a Black boy whose momma is a famous female baseball pitcher, and they want to burn me to death.

The image of Sweeper and his crippled sister at the orphanage, waiting to bolt, comes to me. It's not funny. He told me to bolt before the staff learned my name and face, even told me which rock to move so I could crawl under the admin building and escape. Will he and his sis ever leave that hellhole? My laughter stops as fast as it began.

There's not a star in the sky. The wild onions and dandelions I ate earlier make me burp. I creep from the drainage ditch, keeping low to the ground like an Indian brave. Three tall cottonwoods wave at the sky maybe twenty-five yards from the creek. Cottonwoods have lots of leaves, but their branches are brittle and snap off easily. I test each limb as I climb, picking my way to a stout branch that grows out and up, with plenty of leafy sap suckers to hide me.

Maybe now I'll escape the honor of a Firestone necklace, even live long enough to see my Cardinals win the World Series. Maybe I'll make it to Daddy in Kansas, with a great story to tell. Man, oh man, would Sis have a fit if she could see me now, naked, dirty, bruised. Broke. She'd say, *It's what you get for running off from the orphanage.* When I lived with her, before I'd climb on my bike to go sell newspaper subscriptions, she'd look me up and down. *Change your shirt, for God's sake, Frankie. It's dirty.*

I just changed.

Change it again. And surprise the dirt. Use soap and water on your face and neck. You'll still be ugly, but at least you'll be clean.

I think of Daddy. When I get to Kansas, I'll buy us fox-hounds and we'll hunt like usual. Summers, I'll play baseball. Lots of it. That makes me think of Linda and the Kings. I wonder if she pitched a good game today.

I remember what she said to me one night. *You have beautiful eyes, Frankie Clothespin. You'll be a heartbreaker when you grow up.*

My eyes water thinking of her. A bowl of her beef stew would sure hit the spot about now.

34

Making an Out

I must have dozed off in the cold. I wake to jagged lightning streaking the sky. Thunder booms. The air smells like rain. The voices below are loud and clear. I hug the cottonwood as flashlight beams slice the darkness.

"Ayak?"

"Akia."

"Kigy."

"And I thee. I'm yer Kludd. From Illinois." That voice sounds familiar.

"See anything?"

"Hard to spot a darkie in the dark." Lots of laughs at that.

Another voice says, "Heard we had a Kludd comin' from out of state to help us. That you?"

"It is. Glad to be here for a good cause. That's my aim in life. Helpin' when and where I can." They must shake hands because I hear back slaps and *Glad to meetchas*.

A beam of light sweeps the brush under my tree and along the drainage ditch.

"Kludd, Fats Murphy said our Blackie dived in that slough where we killed all them water moccasins last year. Come out the other side with snakes hangin' off him like licorice strips. Fats said he had him trussed tight, that he just puffed up, threw off his ropes and run. Our jigaboo's voodoo-filled fer sure."

The familiar voice says, "That a fact? I talked with Mr. Fats Murphy. A dedicated Knight who got distracted learnin' baseball pitchin' tips. Happens to young men. He used cannin'-jar rubbers on our boy, not rope. Nah, the boy we're lookin' for ain't voodoo possessed neither. That was weeds hangin' from him, not snakes." A flashlight plays on the tracks and he says, "Where do these tracks go?" I know the speaker. Paul! The hybrid-seed-corn salesman who bought me breakfast and gave me a ride back in Illinois. If he's Klan, he sure fooled me.

Someone says, "Track runs through town all the way to Kansas."

Another says, "Bet our boy's there." His light sweeps the trestle.

Paul says, "Nope. Searched it good. Nothin' there 'cept bats and water moccasins. If we're lookin' for who I think we're lookin' for, he'll be hard to find. He's smarter than a darkie, 'cause he ain't one. He's white."

"C'mon, Kludd. Why do ya say that?"

"I got my reasons. First, that colored team and their whore pitcher played our boys 'fore they played y'all. We didn't have enough Citizens to make a stand neither, it bein' summer and all. They didn't have a young animal with 'em then. Week or so later, I give a fine young man a ride. Red hair. Brown eyes. Freckles. Stocky. Like the one we're chasin'. He ain't no Black."

Another lightning flash, followed by thunder. "All due respect, Kludd, darkies lie. Lie and sleep. That's all they do." He gets lots of agreement from others.

These guys don't know the Kings. When they aren't playing baseball, they're practicing baseball or talking baseball—who covers first base on a bunt to third and no one out. How to foul off a pitch until you get one you like, how to hit a curveball, how to lead off first base so the pitcher balks. That sort of thing. Like Daddy before his stroke, they don't sleep much either.

Someone says, "Our blackie told Fats his mammy were that wench pitcher, Kludd."

"That a fact? Ya ask 'round to see if she birthed any animals?"

"No, sir. We know what we know. JP Ettler seen him with them heathens when he went to spread the gospel. Our boy was at the pitchin' demonstration Friday whoopin' and a hollerin', cheerin' for his momma. JP said he melted through them train wheels like butter when he took off."

"That a fact? Knights, I tell ya. I looked Ettler in the eye. He's lyin' to cover his own mistakes. Tryin' to make hisself look good. Made him take me to where he said he found our boy, and where he escaped. Men, I'm tellin' ya true, that feller got loose 'cause JP Ettler used a persimmon yoke, not oak like you and I woulda done." He pauses. "You Knights is smart. Y'all know JP Ettler didn't go to that camp to spread no gospel. He went there to wet his willy." His cigarette goes brighter.

Someone says, "Went to collect his due, Kludd. That's all."

Paul says, "JP Ettler's a good supporter fer sure. We need his kind, but this ain't 'bout what he done, but the man he is. Think on it. Ya ever hear him quote the Good Book? Hell, he couldn't name the four gospels of the New Testament when I asked him to."

His cigarette glows bright again. No one speaks. "Ya know like I do, that JP wanted that gal pitcher's brown sugar. I ain't bein' critical. She's a looker, all right. Still and all, there's a time and place for a man to enjoy the pleasures of a woman. Men like me and you don't need to break into a tent to do it. We'd get her on the road. Maybe buy her a Nehi. Leave her two dollars. Whatever. I ask ya agin, ya ever see Ettler clean up Saturday night for Sunday morning worship? Ever see him anywhere Sunday mornin' 'cept hungover in his pickup 'neath a tree, sick as poisoned dog?"

No one speaks. "Ya know why he ain't here now? 'Cause he's jist a supporter. Which we need. But JP ain't a man of action like y'all. If he were, he'd be here helpin' us search, not claimin' a Black boy melted like butter 'fore a train engine and disappeared."

A cigarette arcs through the air, bounces off the railroad trestle, and falls into the water. "As yer Kludd, I've certain spiritual obligations. It's my duty to look at every opportunity we got to spread the word, see it from all angles. Make sure it conforms to ritual. See to it we administer the right punishment for the right crime. It's my responsibility as well to pass my spiritual learnin' on to future leaders like y'all. I figger the reason that our boy said he were the Black pitcher's son was to throw y'all a curve. Give ya a taste of somethin' ya want to believe, hopin' ya'd relax and not watch his every move. Worked, didn't it?" Paul's voice is low. "Knights, times are changin'. Today, ya can't jist grab up a darkie, even if they deserve it, and hang a Firestone necklace on him. Today, ya got yer newspaper reporters. Yer radio folks. That damn television, spewing lies. Asshole politicians talkin' about a darkie's civil rights. Even school integration."

He pauses. A match flares. The smell of cigarette smoke fills my nose. Paul's voice is low. I really concentrate to hear him. "Mind ya. I ain't sayin' our boy shouldn't get a life lesson fer fraternizin' with Blacks. It just ain't a necklace offense."

The way Paul says "life lesson" makes me want to skip that honor. Lightning rips the black sky. Thunder rumbles like Daddy's wagon crossing a wooden bridge.

Paul says, "Looks like we got us a toad strangler comin', Citizens. I 'preciate y'all's dedication. Makes me right proud to affiliate with such good men, I tell ya. Yer doin' Christian work that needs doin'. But this ain't the boy to hang a necklace on." He claps his hands. "We got a long week ahead of us. Let's go home. Leave the night to God."

"If ya say so," someone says. "After we check th' trestle." A beam of light sweeps the rusted bridge.

"Be my guest," Paul says. "Watch out fer water moccasins. Don't wanna wake up a sawbones this late at night for somethin' as minor as cuttin' water-moccasin fangs from a Knight's leg." He laughs. "That's wisdom I freely share."

The Knights must talk among themselves because a minute later, someone says, "If ya say ya done a good search, that's 'nuff fer us. We'll head on home."

Paul says, "Yer welcome to double search. I looked in them brush piles. Climbed ever piece of iron. Shined my light in every nook and cranny. Nothin' there but mud dauber nests and bats. Saw nary a snake, but that don't mean they ain't there. Be my guest. Check again."

"Nah, Kludd, you been square with us, so we're satisfied."

I hear back slaps. "Thanks fer yer counsel, Kludd. Much obliged."

Paul says, "Orion, Knights."

One by one, they answer, "Orion."

The lightning's closer now, the wind stronger. Colder. I shiver. Goosebumps cover me. Leaves don't give off much warmth. I step to a lower limb, testing it before putting my full weight on it. A couple more and I'll jump down. My right foot on a thick branch, I go slow, but the limb breaks, and I tumble through the air and land hard, spread-eagled in weeds and mud, unable to breathe. I wheeze and cough, trying to get my lungs to work. My left leg throbs with pain. I push leaves and limbs away and stand. My leg's on fire but seems to work. Bright light hits my eyes, blinding me. It's Firestone-necklace time after all.

PART V

Some people say that baseball is a slow game. The true fan knows a lot happens that many don't see, like who'll cover a base, or the hit and run that puts men on first and third. Little things change the game—an infield hit, a sacrifice bunt. A game can change in a matter of one pitch—a home run, catcher picking a runner off base, a steal of home. The tempo of a contest can change in a heartbeat. What's slow about that?

—Cal Griffin, Hall of Fame team owner.

35

STEALING HOME

"I'll be damned. If it ain't Franklin Delano Walker, Boy Pitching Coach, he who teaches fat third basemen how to pitch." The voice behind the flashlight belongs to Paul, the hybrid-seed corn salesman, and Ku Klux Klan Kludd. "Gotta get ya outta here, boy. Hurry. My car's this way."

I run to catch up. I'm bare-assed. My feet burn. If there were a creek with cold water nearby, I'd jump in and stay there. Paul pushes me into the back seat of his car. Raindrops big as quail eggs bounce off the windshield. Paul starts his car. We jolt down a dirt road, trees scraping the sides of his Chevy, the wind blowing like Dixie.

"Figgered ya'd follow the railroad," Paul says. "Looked fer ya in the trestle, though I figgered you'd know the Knights had that covered. When I seen them cottonwoods, I knew that's where ya were."

The rain is white in the car's headlights. I'm burning up I'm so hot. I roll down the window and stick my feet outside.

Paul says, "Stay in the car, boy." He hands me an RC Cola. "Drink. Ya need the sugar. Ya got hypothermia. Ya feel hot though yer really cold. There's a blanket on the seat. Pull it over ya." He eyes me in the rearview mirror. "Folks would think I'm a pervert if they saw ya."

He whips the car around a wind-fallen tree. "Yer tough as hickory and smart as a raven. No white boy should ever endure what ya have the last day or so."

He hands me a Baby Ruth. "Eat. Once the sugar hits, ya'll feel better. When the rain slows, I'll get yer duds outta my trunk. Found 'em where ya let that stupid Ettler sneak up on ya. He musta figgered ya didn't need clothes fer a Firestone-necklace party." He laughs. I don't know what he finds so funny.

"Back home, I'm a sworn deputy sheriff. Called that St. Louis orphanage you spoke of in that capacity. They said a Franklin Delano Walker visited their facility but left with his guardian after a hour or so." He cackles. "Wouldn't be good to say a new admit escaped his first night, now would it?"

He lights a Chesterfield, steering the car in rain and wind with his knees. "Citizens down here thought ya was a darkie 'cause ya was with that colored ball team. A natural mistake. Still, they should've asked 'round 'fore they nabbed ya."

He sighs. "And you. Ya gotta learn Blacks are Blacks and ya gotta leave 'em alone. I realize good baseball players blind us all. I'll chalk yer indiscretions up to bein' young and dumb."

He waves his hand in front of the car's heater. "Feelin' better? We'll go to my sister, Becky's, in Seneca. She'll know what to do with ya."

Becky's house is just off US 43 in Seneca, Missouri. Paul bangs on the door. "Got a boy I pulled from a celebration," he says.

"Thought you'd quit the Klan," Becky says. She looks at me like I'm a lost puppy. "You need a bath. Then I'll dab Mercurochrome on your cuts. You poor thing." She starts water running in the tub.

"He's a tough one," Paul says. Then, says, "I quit. Till them Mexicans started takin' jobs from 'mericans. That woke me up. Rejoined. Got elected Kludd. Which is good. Figger I can be a voice of reason in bad situations. Improve the bad rep the Klan has for defendin' white folks' rights."

"Sorry you waste your time with that bunch. They about killed an innocent boy. Doesn't that bother you?"

"Proves my point. It was me who kept things from goin' bad to worse."

"My eyes are closed," she says as she hands me a towel. She leaves me in the bathroom, but I can hear them talking.

"Before we divorced," Becky says to Paul, "Blake did a study that said the Klan had about died out around here. Was he wrong?"

Paul ignores Becky's question. "White folks need to be alert to the rights they're losin' or soon they won't have none to lose. What we gonna do with Mr. Franklin Delano Walker?"

"White folks losing rights is a lame argument that's been used for years. Name me one right white folks have lost in the past twenty years."

Paul doesn't answer. Becky slaps his shoulder. "See? You can't. You're just against colored is all. Just like Daddy." Becky is quiet for a second, then says, "Restaurant's closed every Wednesday. Parsons is a short drive. I'll drive him over then. Okay?"

She speaks to me through the bathroom door. "You know your sister's address?"

The skin I scraped falling from the cottonwood stings. "Parsons, Kansas, is all I know."

"We'll ask at the post office. You know her name, right?"

"Pardee. Carolina Pardee."

Paul says, "Sounds okay for me. Get the boy to his daddy's. He's had a hard trip."

He comes to the bathroom door. "I got a million things to do and a long drive home, Franklin Delano Walker. Quite a moniker." He laughs. "Ya deserve a break or two. I'll tell the Citizens in Joplin to cool it. They were after the wrong boy for the wrong crime. You can come and go, no problem. Hope to see ya play ball sometime."

Becky says, "If I have my way and he wants to, he can play ball night and day."

It sure beats being the honored guest at a Firestone-necklace party, I tell you.

Becky leads me to a room with a single bed, clean white sheets, and a blue wool blanket. I'm asleep before my head hits the pillow. I don't dream, but I do hear Becky slip in quiet as a cat and put something on the chair next to the bed. Later, her car chugs to life and headlights streak the wall above my bed. She's off to work, I figure.

Sparrows squabbling in the tree outside bring me awake. I smell Mercurochrome. My whole right side where I scraped off skin is painted red, as are the small cuts on my legs and arms. Becky's been busy. How did I sleep through that?

My old jeans and shirt are folded neatly on the chair. I pull them on and go outside, get my bearings. Becky's house is magazine pretty, sitting on a big green lawn beneath tall maples. Red and white roses bloom along a wire fence, with each post painted green.

Last night she gave me directions and told me to come eat breakfast when I woke up, so I trot off to her café. When I get there I'm surprised by the way her back porch looks. Weeds grow knee high along the sidewalk. Cardboard boxes, half broken down, are piled against a whitewashed building. Empty milk and soda pop bottles litter the grass. Her trash can looks like it hasn't been emptied for weeks, much less burned. The sidewalk needs hosing off.

If Sis were here, she'd say, *Grab a broom, Frankie. When you've got things looking better, go ask for money to finish the job. You can make your rent on this one job.*

I sweep up trash and put it in the burn barrel and separate Coke, Dr. Pepper, RC Cola, and milk bottles, then put them in their cases. Next, I stack the return crates next to the white building, grab a reap hook from the tool shed, and go to work on the weeds along the sidewalk.

A guy with a thin mustache, hair slicked back and parted in the middle, a short apron with food stains tied at his waist, comes out and lights a Camel. "What the hell?"

"Cleaning up so you'll pass the food inspector's visit." Sis told me restaurant owners worry about this.

He nods and goes back inside. A few minutes later, Becky comes out. She wipes away tears with a yellow and blue handkerchief. "Jeremy used to keep this area clean for me. When he was no longer...available, I hired a high-school boy. He graduated in June. I put off hiring someone else for some reason."

She pats my shoulder. "Breakfast or dinner when you finish? Meatloaf is today's special. Or chicken-fried steak and gravy?"

After the lunch-hour rush ends Becky says, "C'mon. Let's go tell the sheriff what happened to you."

The sign outside the police department says this is the sheriff's auxiliary office. It's no bigger that an outhouse and smells of chewing tobacco and pipe smoke. "Sheriff's out, pretty lady," the deputy says. "Tell me what brings you out this fine day. Rest assured, I'll make a formal report to the Big Man if yer story deserves consideration."

His desk takes up most of the room. He sits in a black swivel chair with a blue cushion. We sit in straight-back chairs against the wall. "Glad to see ya, Miss Becky. Ya look pretty as always." He winks at me. "How may I be of service to ya?"

She says, "This is Franklin Walker. He was kidnapped by the KKK. He has a story to tell." She nods at me.

I say, "Two big guys grabbed me at the Greyhound station and threw me into their pickup, I got loose…" The deputy waves his hand and picks up a yellow notebook.

"A Mr. Paul Roberts done reported this incident. He's a agriculture specialist at that college in Cape Girardeau. An' a sworn deputy. Badge and all. He said—"

Becky laughs. "Paul Roberts? A college professor? Never. He's my brother. He sells seed corn. He's not an *agricultural specialist*."

The deputy ignores this. "Said he was supervisin' a bunch of college boys on a campin' trip. One team grabbed a young man as a joke and hid him to prove to the other team they were smarter and tougher. Mr. Roberts hisself said he personally delivered the boy to a relative who'll return him to his family. Said it was all a silly college prank." The deputy shakes his head. "Book learnin' don't keep young men from doin' stupid things."

"You were lied to," Becky says. "Paul Roberts is a Ku Klux Klan member."

"Now, missy, hold on. Yer own husband—ex-husband now, I reckon—said in his quite expensive and comprehensive report that he presented to all of us law enforcement officers, that the Klan's gone from these parts. Yer ex is a big state highway patrol officer, not a Johnny Jump Up county deputy like me."

It's Becky turn to ignore words. "That was years ago. My brother, Paul Roberts, lives in Illinois. The KKK called him to come officiate at a ritual where they planned to hang a burning car tire around this boy's neck. That proves they're active here." She taps my shoulder. "Tell him about the camp where you were held."

I know the deputy won't listen to what I have to say. He's like Sis. He hears only what he wants to hear. Still, I give it a try. "Fats Murphy, third baseman on the local ball team, and this other goon grabbed me in the Greyhound station and dragged me out to a pickup truck, tied my hands behind me with canning jar rubbers, and drove me to a camp. It's on a hill above a slough. Near the railroad tracks. A brush arbor out front. Three tall chairs face a fire pit. Green benches for people to sit on. Two privies out back. They were gonna give me a Firestone necklace."

The deputy smiles. "You described Christian Camp in the Woods to a tee. Ever church hereabouts uses it fer baptisms. Revivals. Whatever. No Klan activity there, just a place for good Christians to worship."

I'd like to answer the way Klan Kludd Paul sometimes does. *Is that a fact?* Instead, I say, "I gave Fats Murphy some pitching tips. A minister brought him fried chicken. A back. Two wings. Fats kept asking for relief from guarding me so he could make deliveries. His wife needs twenty bucks bad this week."

The deputy sighs. "A little young to know much 'bout pitchin', ain't ya? But we sure do need a good arm." He inspects his fingernails. "I know Fats Murphy. Good Christian man. Owns a three-quarter-ton truck. Delivers most anything for a fair price. Wife keeps his nose to the grindstone. Most men need that." He smiles at Becky. "As you know."

I'd like to punch his red face.

"Fats married my cousin Naomi, twice removed. Nice girl. A little bossy." He pulls a plug of tobacco from his pocket and cuts a chaw with a pearl-handled knife. "No doubt about it. You was nabbed by college boys feelin' their oats, impersonatin' the KKK. Seemed real to ya, bein' young and all. But as we know from that comprehensive highway patrol report this here lady's ex-husband wrote, the Klan don't operate 'round here." He shrugs. "College. Waste of time and money, ya ask me."

He winks at Becky and clambers to his feet. "Thanks for comin' by, pretty lady. We like community folks to be involved in law enforcement issues. I'll tell the sheriff the pretty café owner dropped in with a interestin' story that don't jive with our official report. That the boy who says he was nabbed is safe. Paul Roberts did as he said and turned the youngster over to his own kin, unharmed. Sheriff may or may not investigate. His call."

Before Becky can speak, he says, "I'll for sure let him know Deputy Paul Roberts is yer brother. If'n it matters. Anything more I can do fer ya, we're here to serve." He taps his cowboy hat in place and kinda pushes us toward the door.

In the car, Becky says, "That SOB. He won't say one word to the sheriff."

She digs her fists into her temple. "Called me a pretty girl. I'm a grown woman, for God's sake. Besides, what do my looks have to do with a young boy being kidnapped?" She gives a short laugh. "Paul Roberts a professor? Then I'm Kate Smith and I can't carry a tune in a fruit basket."

36

Batting Average

On Wednesday, with her café closed, Becky drives me to Parsons. On the way she tells me about Jeremy, her son. "He was your age. Eleven. He and his best friend, Leo, drank chocolate milk on my back porch after school, jumped on their bikes, and took off like they'd done hundreds of times." Her face is pale. Her voice low. She seems far away. "I was making apple butter. Didn't watch which way they went, north or south. Wednesday. September 15, 1949. Four twenty-five in the afternoon. Never saw either of them again. Jeremy was my only child. Our only child, I should say. I was married then to Blake."

I watch the highway disappear under the car.

Becky goes on. "No one knows what happened to them. The Highway Patrol Special Unit searched for three weeks. Day and night. Detectives from St. Louis and Chicago came. Carloads of experts on finding missing people. The patrol investigated their disappearance for a year. Not one trace was ever found. No bikes. No clothing. Nothing. Poof. They just vanished."

She glances at me with dry eyes. "Blake reviews the evidence book every day he works. He's searched every cave for miles around. Hikes these hills looking for a scrap of clothing, abandoned bike, anything that could be theirs." She says this like she's reporting she ran out of milk at her café. "Maybe they went to explore a cave and a rockslide sealed the entrance. There're dozens of caves in these hills. Maybe they went to watch those fancy earth movers dig the new highway, fell in a ditch...I've prayed every day for two years for God to bring them home. Jeremy was special in so many ways. But I know he won't come home. Now I pray for a second chance to be a mother."

She has tears now, but she smiles. "Maybe you're God's answer to me." She squeezes my shoulder. I watch trees whiz by.

Becky turns to face me, her brown eyes wide. "Forgive me. I shouldn't have said that. I'm not a nutcase, Frankie. Really." She shakes her head and licks her lips. "You got good home training somewhere. You're polite. Considerate. Easy to be around. I'd be happy if you'd consider letting me adopt you."

She touches my hand. "You're levelheaded. You cleaned up that mess behind my café without asking one question."

I don't know what to say, so I just sit there, watching the big clouds overhead.

"You'd have your own room. Clothes. We'd buy one of those television sets they advertise in the newspaper. Get a dog if you want. School's just three blocks away." She laughs. "Fair warning. I'm a stickler about homework."

She squeezes my hand. "Mainly, you'd just be a boy. Play baseball. Swim. Fish. Grow into a fine man." Her eyes lock on mine. "If things don't work out with your family, and I pray they do, give me a call. Please."

In Parsons, Becky gets direction to my sister's house from the post office. She parks across the street, kisses my hand, and pushes a paper and five one-dollar bills into my shirt pocket. "You need anything, call. Day or night. I'm here for you."

She points at the Band-Aid on my elbow. "Keep that on for two, three more days." The Mercurochrome she smeared on me has about worn off. My throat hurts and it's hard to swallow.

"Thanks," I mumble, hug her neck, and step into full sunshine under a blue sky. The house I've chased since I bolted from the orphanage is a white two-story. Four bare windows face west. Wire fence. Unpainted posts. Lawn needs mowing. Concrete sidewalk leading from the yard to the porch. Oleander bushes. A green porch swing moves in the wind. The house could use a paint job.

Becky bought me some Golden Grain tobacco and box of Cracker Jacks in Seneca. Daddy's favorites. I take them from my sack. She said, *Always take a gift when you visit someone the first time.*

A woman answers my knock. When Becky sees this, she honks and drives off.

"You, Carolina?"

The brown-haired lady who must be my sister looks me up and down. "Frankie? Why'd you come here?"

"To see Daddy. I have his pipe." I lost my ball glove the night the KKK chased me, but Daddy's pipe was with the clothes Paul found.

"He doesn't need that smelly ol' thing." Carolina opens the door.

The front room is dark, but I see a sofa, a rocking chair, a tall radio against one wall, and a round rug on a hardwood floor. A pile of diapers on the sofa. A tricycle and a doll with no hair are in the hallway.

Carolina says, "Ginny told me the orphanage said you weren't there." Carolina shakes her head. "I had no idea…" She fights tears. "She put you there till you learned to stop lying. Grow up. She'd come get you after a month or so."

I nod. Talk about lies.

Carolina points to a closed door. "Daddy's in there."

I'm ready to talk foxhunting and baseball and eat Cracker Jacks with Daddy.

She picks up the doll and pushes the tricycle down the hall. "I'll call Ginny at work. She'll be glad to know where you are. Be sure to write her tomorrow, hear?"

Daddy's room is dim and smells of sweat and sun-warmed wood. He sits in a straight-backed chair next to an open window. His cot is unmade. Cold blue eyes. Overalls gallous unhooked. No shirt, gray chest hair against gray skin. No shoes. No socks. His toenails need cutting. A radio on the floor spews church music. When I lean in to kiss him, he doesn't move.

"I have your pipe." I press it into his snow-cold hand. His fingers don't close around it. When I take my hand away, it falls to the floor. There'll be no foxhunting or baseball talk, I guess.

After supper, certainly not as good as Linda fixed for the Kings, Carolina asks, "Frankie, how long do you plan on staying? I made you a pallet in Daddy's room."

Harold, her husband, says, "Let the boy rest a day or two before ya pepper him with questions. St. Louis is a long way from here." If only he knew.

Carolina sighs. "I've got four little ones. Two in school. Two still in diapers."

Harold touches her hand. "I know." He slaps my shoulder. "Never mind her. You're welcome here."

"For a week or so," Carolina says. She jumps up and goes into the kitchen.

What did my baseball pitching friend Linda say? *Your sister may not want another mouth to feed.* She was right. As usual.

I go down the hall to Daddy's room and hear Harold say, "You see the bruise on that boy's back? He's been through some hard stuff."

"Remember, he lies a lot. That's why Ginny put in him in the orphanage," Carolina says.

"The marks on his body didn't get there from lies."

The next morning Carolina's four little ones are at the breakfast table. Two blond-headed, blue-eyed girls in diapers, a first-grader daughter, and a brown-haired boy, eight or nine years old. I don't know their names. They look at me like I have two heads. I pour Rice Krispies into a bowl, add milk and sugar, peel a banana, and slice it with a table knife, pushing each piece off the blade with my thumb.

"Momma," the boy yells, "your brother's so dumb he doesn't know how to slice a banana."

Carolina's in the kitchen. "Frankie, do it right," she calls.

I make sure the boy watches and plop the whole banana into my bowl.

"Shit. He's gonna eat the whole thin'. Come look, Momma."

Carolina comes in and slaps his hand. "No cussing. You sound like you don't have a momma." She looks at me when she says this. I guess that puts me in my place. "Behave, Frankie. Use your manners. If you have any." Back in the kitchen, she calls, "Darling, come get your eggs."

Her son doesn't move, he's so intrigued by me. I mash the banana with my spoon and add milk.

"Yech," he says.

"That's gross," his older sister chimes in.

"Jarrod. Your eggs are ready," Carolina calls. Her son hurries to the kitchen. He's back in a flash. He starts to sit. I hook my toe around his chair leg and tug. Jarrod misses his seat and sprawls to the floor, plate flying, bacon and eggs sliding across the linoleum floor.

He cries, "Frankie made me do it. He moved my chair."

"You can't blame everything on Frankie," Carolina says. "Clean up your mess. Hurry. Or you'll be late for the park."

Carolina hands a dish rag and towel to Jarrod. I've finished my cereal. "May I be excused?" I ask. Sis taught me that.

Carolina's eyes go big. "Why...why of course."

Daddy is on his cot, his sheet and blanket wadded beneath his bare legs. He looks stiff as a hickory limb. Again, Little Linda threw a strike. Daddy's certainly not the same man as before his stroke. All at once I feel tired. Real tired. I sit on Daddy's cot and lay my head on his chest. Tears fill my eyes and spill onto Daddy's shoulder. I try to stop the tears by pushing at my eyes, but they keep coming. They run down my cheeks, so salty that I gag. No matter how I try to stop their flow, they come. I sob. My body shakes. My chest heaves.

I cry for all the times Daddy and I chased the moon following our foxhounds. I cry for the stroke that paralyzed him. I cry for the best foxhound I've ever known, my Dinah, and now she's gone. I cry for Sis and the nights she searches beer joint after beer joint, hoping to drag Hubby home while he's sober enough to walk. I cry for Hubby and his silly poems and the funny names he gives people. I cry for Sweeper and Claudia waiting to bolt from the orphanage. I cry for hybrid-seed corn salesman and KKK Kludd Paul, who saved me from a Firestone necklace and took me to Becky's. I cry for Little Linda and how her eyes gleam when she winds to pitch. I cry for Pops Buell and the Kings' barnstorming team and the death of that Grand Tradition. I cry for clumsy third baseman Fats Murphy, who wants to be a pitcher and his wife who needs twenty bucks. I cry for Becky and her son, Jeremy, who never came home from a bicycle ride. I cry for my Cardinals and the hundreds of imaginary games I've played in my head. I cry for my nephew Jarrod who I just sent sprawling this morning. I cry because I lie when the truth would be better. I cry because I don't know where or when I'll go to school, where I'll live, or where I'll eat my next meal.

I cry and cry, tears wetting my face, snot running like a yellow fountain, my shoulders jerking, my face aching. I cry and cry. Finally, so tired I can hardly move, my tears stop. I fall asleep on Daddy's stomach, him as cold and silent as a tombstone in a cemetery.

37

RUNS BATTED IN

Carolina is peeling potatoes at the kitchen sink when I come in. The radio's tuned to *Young Dr. Malone*. It smells like fish and steam.

"Have a wash pan?"

She raises her eyebrows and nods at the pantry. I find a white enamel basin, fill it with hot water, grab scissors from the sewing machine in the hall, take a towel and washcloth from the bathroom, and go to Daddy. He sits in the chair next to the cot, his blue, bare feet on the wood floor.

"This will be hot," I say, putting first his right foot, then his left into the hot water. I drape the towel over his shoulders. Pretending I'm a barber, I say, "So, Mick. Had any good foxhunts lately?"

I know he can't answer. I push a Cracker Jack into his mouth. He gums it silently.

"Good, huh?"

I wait until Daddy's swallowed several kernels, wet the washcloth, and wash his thin white hair. While it's still damp I trim his hair, sawing away the bristles around his ears, and clipping his bushy eyebrows.

Using the washcloth I soak his whiskers, then lather his face. When white foam hides his pale face, I shave him, stopping the blood from any nicks with toilet paper. Then I wash and dry his feet, trim his toenails, and pull socks over his blue feet and stuff them into his slippers.

When Daddy could talk, he'd joke, "I'm country and always will be country. You can put lipstick on your hog, it'll still be a hog." Now, I say, "You look like a rich farmer. You ever foxhunt any?" I know he won't answer, but I've nothing else to do.

Daddy closes his eyes. He's tired. I help him to a rocker on the front porch. "You can watch the sparrows and robins."

Back inside, I stuff a spare shirt, change of socks, and clean jeans into the flour sack I found in the smokehouse. Time to hit the road.

Carolina raps on the door. "Ginny's on the telephone. She has news you'll like."

I lift the receiver. Sis sounds far away. "All that discipline at the orphanage too much for you?"

I don't answer. She says, "Your manager at the *Sun-Gazette* came looking for you. And your ball team manager. Said you were in Kansas. What'd I know? You didn't have the decency to tell me where you were." Here comes my ass chewing. Instead she says, "Folks tell me I'm too hard on you. Maybe they're right."

I didn't expect that. I hear her swallow.

"This will come as no surprise, but Thomas and I are getting a divorce." It takes me a minute to remember that's Hubby's name.

"I read that pamphlet and magazine article you brought home. Thomas won't go to their meetings. I talked with some sober men and their wives. They said he has to want to stop drinking or AA, or any other cure, won't work."

She blows her nose. "He says he sees nothing wrong with a drink or two after a day's work. AA people say if he's an alcoholic he has to stop drinking. Period." She swallows again. "He's killing himself. I can't watch that."

I don't say anything. She sobs. My eyes are wet too.

Her voice is hoarse when she next speaks. "My Greyhound gets in at 4:17 day after tomorrow." Another pause. "Can we start over? Me and you? If I promise to loosen up? Let you play ball? Maybe you could get a different job, not sell newspaper subscriptions? Be a busboy? Set pins in a bowling alley? Something that's easier on us both."

I clear my throat. "Can I eat peanut butter?"

"Sure. So the ants won't get it." She giggles.

"I'll meet your bus."

We hang up.

I go into Daddy's room, get the box of Cracker Jacks, pull the five singles from my pocket, and go to the kitchen where Carolina and Harold drink coffee.

Carolina asks, "Great news about Ginny, huh?"

I don't answer. I lay a dollar on the table. "Here's a buck for my bed." I lay down another buck. "For my eats." I hand her the box of Cracker Jack. "For your kids. Sis and I'll be rooming together, so I'll be here another week."

I lay down three more bucks. "Is five dollars a week enough rent?"

Harold hands the money back. "Family's welcome in my house. No charge." He smiles. "Saw you dolled your dad up good. Looks like a new man."

He taps my shoulder. "You're tough as boot leather, and smart. In exchange for rent money, your sister might have a chore or two for you. Figure you'll need a job. You can start looking tomorrow."

He hands me a ball glove and ball. "Dug these out of the attic. Bat's on the porch. I played a mean second base when I was younger. What say I hit you some grounders?"

38

WINNING PITCHER

I found a busboy job at Henderson's Café on Main Street in Parsons the next day. A week later Sis hired on to demonstrate Singer sewing machines at county fairs, carnivals, and places where people congregate. She'll travel some, which she says will keep us out of each other's hair. She gets paid a salary plus commissions, so she feels fat and happy, I reckon.

We rented a furnished three-room apartment with a kitchen, a bedroom, and a living room with a couch where I sleep. Fifty-five smackers a month, utilities paid. Harold and I hit each other grounders two or three nights before I moved. He's a pretty good fielder, but no Bob Tharp, the Kings' leading hitter at the plate. Sis nags me from morning to night to do my homework. She won't let me go out for football now that fall's coming on.

Nights, I often think of my time with the Kings. This brings me face to face with the Firestone necklace the KKK planned to give me. I wonder what would have happened if Paul Roberts, the KKK's Kludd, hadn't rescued me. I guess he's in Illinois now. And I think of Linda, the Kings pitcher in Omaha. I should write her but I know I won't.

Still, it's Sweeper and his sister, Claudia, I think of most. How do I pay him back for his help? With his back to me so we wouldn't get caught fraternizing, he said, *My name's Fredrick T. Oates. Ya don't know me from a dick on a dog, but I been here more 'n a year. I know a thing or two.* He sure did.

One Sunday morning before I go in to set pins at the bowling alley, I use the telephone booth in the lobby and call Paul Roberts. "This is Franklin Delano Walker. You said call if I needed something."

"Hey, Boy Baseball Pitching Coach. Fall outta any trees lately?"

I ignore this and get down to business. "At the orphanage, a boy named Freddie Oates gave me tips on what to expect and showed me how to bolt from that evil place. I want to send him a box of cookies as thanks."

A lie, yes, but maybe God will forgive me. "In your capacity as a sworn deputy could you find out if he's still there? His sister's name is Claudia."

"A box of cookies, huh? Comin' from you, I know there's more to it than just cookies." He gives a short laugh. "Whatcha got planned? No. Don't tell me. Okay. Let me git a pencil." He grunts. "Aw right. How ya spell his name?"

I spell Fredrick T. Oates and give Paul Carolina's number to telephone me back when he finds out about Sweeper. "If I'm not there, leave a message, okay?"

When I'm off work I telephone Becky, my good friend who opened her home to me. She answers on the first ring.

"Frankie, you okay?"

"I'm fine, thanks."

"I worry about you. School going okay? Doing your homework?"

"Mostly." I get right to the reason for my call. "I need a favor." I lay it on a little thick, talking about Sweeper—Freddie Oates. Saying he's a friend who helped me get settled at the orphanage and would make a great boy for her to adopt.

"Can we go get him out of that prison? I have eleven dollars for gas."

"Oh, Frankie, there's no need for that. I'll pay for everything. Gas. The travel court. Meals. Why do you think Freddie would be a good match for me?"

That's an easy one. "He's smart and well-mannered."

The next day, I bike out to Carolina's. I'm hardly through the door before she says, "A Deputy Sheriff Paul Roberts telephoned, asking for you. I took a message." Her face is pale. She looks at her notepad. "He said, 'Fredrick T. Oates still resides at the orphanage. No record of his sister Claudia.' What's this about, Frankie?"

"Freddie's my friend. I wanna send him cookies for his birthday. Ginny said it was okay."

She smiles. "That's right nice of you, Frankie. Why's the deputy involved?"

"I met him on the road. His ministry is to help orphans. If I called, Admin would never let me know if Freddie was there or not. But they'll answer any question the deputy asks. You understand?"

"Your common sense is a surprise sometimes, Frankie."

Intake officer Brother Tipton is behind his desk when Becky and I come into the Missouri Orphan's School and Residence. He wears his thin green suspenders with the red stripe today, plus his usual white socks and black shoes.

Fredrick T. Oates comes in looking like he just woke up. His hair is shaved short, his eyes the same washed-out brown. He walks with a shuffle. If he remembers me, he doesn't let on.

"I'm your aunt," Becky says. "Your daddy's sister."

"Didn't know I had either one," Sweeper says.

"You do, dear." The orphanage is used to things like this. Families often leave a kid or two there in the winter and come get them in the springtime for planting season. With Freddie gone, the orphanage has one less mouth to feed. We wait while Becky fills out a long form and signs her name.

In her car, Freddie babbles, "Had a sister when I come here. She went to the infirmary. Never come back. Assholes say she was adopted. Who took her and where, they won't say."

Freddie's smaller than I remember, with buck teeth. More thin than wiry. He babbles, "I got family in Texas. Denton, I hear tell. Me and Claudia was aimin' to go there, but she never come back to the girls' ward. Went to the infirmary to see her, they said she were in class. Don't believe it. When I get to Texas, I'll buy me a horse. Blue jeans. Cowboy hat. Get me a job." He watches the scenery go by. "Wonder who'll clean commodes at the Home with me gone?"

Becky says, "The paper I signed calls for me to bring you back in six months if it doesn't work between you and me. You understand that?"

Freddie nods. "I reckon. Never been adopted afore. Admin says my older sister Claudia was. But I ask you, who'd want a gangly sixteen-year-old crippled by polio?' He answers his own question. "Nobody, that's who."

We stop in St. Charles for food. When the waitress brings our order, Freddie puts his arms around his plate like he's protecting it from attack. He gobbles his hamburger and french fries almost before I get ketchup on my cheeseburger. Becky looks straight ahead, a small smile glued to her face.

When we stop for gas, Freddie washes all her windshields, checks the oil and tire pressure, and sweeps the car floorboards with a whisk broom.

"Thank you, Fredrick," Becky says.

"Freddie Oates at yer service. A soda pop would sure hit the spot."

"Certainly. So you won't have to ask me when you want a treat, here's a dollar. Buy what you want."

"A whole dollar? Never had one all to myself afore."

Becky smiles, looks at me, and shakes her head. "There's no substitute for home training." Becky seems in a hurry now, speeding through small towns, past farmhouses and white barns; some of these could be what I passed the night I bolted. We stop only for gas, restroom breaks, and snacks.

At my apartment in Parsons, she says, "Franklin Walker, you're a wonder. I'll telephone you at work in a day or two to tell you how things are going."

Ginny isn't home, so I have the place to myself. I fry up bacon and eggs, toast two slices of bread in the oven, eat, and hit the hay. The fair season is over, so she comes home Tuesday. She doesn't know I've been gone. She's gaga over her new man.

"He's a social drinker," she says. "Handsome. Smooth

dancer. Drives a snazzy De Soto Custom four-door." She'll demonstrate her Singer sewing machines at Sears and JCPenney in Pittsburg, Kansas, until Christmas.

Two days before Thanksgiving, I come home from work. Who's sitting on my doorstep? None other than Freddie Oates.

"Hey, Jetsie. How ya been?" He follows me inside. "Come by to say so long. Goin' to Texas. Me and Miss Becky? Well, let's say it ain't a go. I'm not much on school learnin' and not a churchgoin' man." He kinda laughs. "You can clean up stuff 'round her café just so often."

He pulls a Dr. Pepper from his front pocket along with a Grapette. "Let's have a toast. We is both out of th' orphanage. I'm on my way to kin in Texas with a twenty-dollar bill in my pocket, an' you got yerself a good job an' a roof over yer head. I'd say we're doin' right good, wouldn't you?"

He hit the road the next morning after a breakfast of bacon and eggs, carrying a sack with a change of underwear and socks, two peanut butter and jelly sandwiches, and the clothes on his back. The last I saw, he was standing by the highway, his thumb out, wanting a ride to Texas. The last thing he said to me was, "I betcha Claudia's there. They come and adopted her. You just watch." I never heard from him again.

In February, Sis married her social drinker man, and I rented a room at Madame Sassie von Wolfe's Edifice for Gentlemen, twenty-five dollars a month. I stayed there till I graduated high school and joined the Marines.

Daddy died in April. We buried him in a cemetery in Parsons, under an oak tree, far from the Ozark hills he loved. Harold, Carolina's husband, came out of retirement and played second base for the Parsons Merchants. I was bat boy until I was big enough to play Little League, followed by high school and Legion baseball. I was a pretty good pitcher but was never able to throw a curveball like Little Linda, baseball's only professional female pitcher, formerly with the Kansas City River Kings and Mississippi Mud Dogs all-star baseball team.

Once a month I spend a day or two with Becky in Seneca. Summers, after ball season, we go camping for a week. She never mentions Jeremy, her lost son, or her brother, Paul Roberts, of the Ku Klux Klan. The night I graduated high school she took me to dinner.

"I sold my restaurant. Moving to California. I'm tired of the same thing every day." She pauses. "Who knows, maybe our paths will cross again if you're stationed out there."

Nights in bed I lie real still and listen to the wind blow tree branches against the apartment house. It feels like Daddy and I are following our hounds in the hills once again.

Dinah's sweet liberty-bell mouth echoes along the ridgeline as she drives that fox under a star-filled sky. Water splashes in the creek nearby and a girl with sweet cocoa-colored skin swims toward me. When she surfaces, my life will change.

She taught me life is like baseball: the one who does the little things the best wins. One of these days I'll look her up and say "thank you." We sure have a lot to talk about.

ACKNOWLEDGMENTS

My cup runneth over. This novella would not have happened without the encouragement and support of NPB; Frick, Frack, and MTP all played crucial roles. Michelle Ivy Davis, your suggestions have been invaluable. Clive Gill, your advice and counsel is greatly appreciated. Thanks to Pam Van Dyk, editor par excellence at Regal House Publishing. Patient. Knowledgeable. Understanding. Her advice and dedication made a good story one of excellence. Thank you. A big gob of gratitude also goes to Jaynie Royal, Founder, Regal House Publishing. Her email saying she'd publish "God" came on a day when fish ignored my every lure, Yosemite was on fire, and Covid-19 stalked the universe. Her email gave me hope. Thank you.

CREDITS

The Wit and Wisdom of Satchel Paige, Negro Leagues Baseball Museum, 1964 (used with permission of the publisher)
The Story of Baseball in 100 Photographs, Sports Illustrated, 2019 (used with permission of the publisher)
Casey Stengel Talks Baseball, Doubleday Publishing, 1967
Pitching Wins Championships, Red Rooster Press, 1963

All other quotations are from the private collection of the author.